Rainer Maria Rilke

Two Prague Stories

with an epilogue by Harald Salfellner
and five color illustrations
by Jiří Vincenc Slavíček

Vitalis

D0926224

© Vitalis
© Translation from the German: Isabel Cole
© Cover and illustrations: Jiří Vincenc Slavíček
Typesetting: Cadis, Praha
Printing and binding: Finidr, Český Těšín
All rights reserved

ISBN 80-7253-073-9

Foreword

This book is sheer past. Homeland and child-hood – both of them long remote – form its background. – Today I would not have written it this way, and so I probably would not have written it at all. But back then, when I wrote it, it was necessary for me. It made half-forgotten things dear to me and thus enriched me; for all we possess of the past is that which we love. And we want to possess all that we have experienced.

Rainer Maria Rilke

Schmargendorf, February 1899

King Bohusch

Entering the National Cafe[1] across from Prague's Czech theater at three in the afternoon, the great actor Norinski started, then immediately smiled his most contemptuous smile: the mirror diagonally opposite the door had caught some remote corner of the room, and in it he had glimpsed a crooked marble pillar and beneath this pillar a hunchbacked little man whose strange eyes stared furtively at the newcomer from his misshapen head. The strangeness of his gaze, in whose depths some unimaginable event seemed darkly mirrored, had frightened him momentarily. Not that he was especially apprehensive by nature, no, it was due to the profound and contemplative disposition common to such great artists, a bulwark through which each event must bore its way. Norinski felt nothing of the kind toward the original. He even ignored the hunchback for quite a while as he extended his hand with unnecessary gravity to the other regulars. The handshakes took some time; each had, as it were, three acts. First act: reluctantly the actor's hand gives in to the pleading of the outstretched hands. Second act: his hand speaks

[1] National Café: Rilke is alluding to the Cafe "Slavia" on Národní třída opposite the National Theater.

emphatically to the one it clasps: Do you realize the significance of this moment? Third act and catastrophe, in which Norinski contemptuously dropped, tossed away each hand: Oh you wretched man, how could you realize... The wretched men, this time, were: Karás, the tall pale critic from the *Tschas*[2], distinguished by an extremely long neck and – as a malicious Jewish colleague had once put it – an extremely courteous "Adam's apple" which escorted each drop down through the loneliness of the gullet to the top of the collar, where it could not possibly lose its way, and then darted assiduously back to its post; Schileder, the handsome painter who painted such sad things; the novelist Pátek; the poet Machal; and the student Rezek, who sat somewhat apart, silently drinking hot *Tschaj*[3] with plenty of cognac from a big glass. Finally Norinski seemed to notice the hunchback too. He laughed: "King Bohusch!" and reached his hand across the marble table with an ironic "Majesty". The little man jumped to his feet and, not to keep the Thespian's hand waiting, shot his yellow unripe fingers at him, so that the two hands collided like birds in the air. Bohusch, finding this rather droll, let out a trembling, broken laugh, but stopped fearfully as he saw the pockmarks on Norinski's forehead hide in angry furrows. The Thespian muttered something, gave up the hunt, and said ill-temperedly to Karás:

[2] "Tschas": German spelling of Czech *čas*: "Time" (a journal)

[3] "Tschaj": German spelling of Czech *čaj* = tea

"My good man, you do write some awful rubbish. But I can tell you this, next time I'll play my Hamlet just as I did yesterday. I play *mine*, after all. Understood, my dear fellow?"

Karás took a swallow and said something about the interpretation others had expressed, eminent people; he need only mention Kainz or – the student Rezek drained his glass with vehemence, and Norinski said angrily:

"My dear man, what's a German Hamlet to me? Surely you don't mean to say that we can't have our own opinion? Is Shakespeare German? Well then, why should we bother ourselves with the Germans? I take my interpretation straight from the English, so to speak."

"The only proper thing to do," sanctioned Pátek, stroking his fashionable goatee with well-groomed fingers.

"Your costume, by the way, from an artistic point of view, I mean –" soothed the handsome painter, and Norinski turned to him quickly. "Yes," he yawned ever so carelessly, and then in a patronizing tone:

"How goes the play, Machal?"

The poet gazed silently into his absinthe glass for a while and replied softly and sadly: "It's Spring."

They were all expecting more to come, but evidently the poet was already off to the pale garden of his dreams again. He watched his absinthe glass grow and grow until he felt he himself was in the midst of this opaline light, weightless, utterly dissolved in this singular atmosphere. Only Schileder had taken the tremendous words seriously. They hung over him, so close that he could not have twitched an eyelash. Deep down inside he thought: God, anyone could manage that. Did he say anything out of the ordinary? I can too: it's... He did not finish the thought. Everyone laughed, and Schileder breathed a sigh of relief as he saw from the other's faces that the statement could not have been so momentous after all. Karás turned to the poet: "So that means your play is blossoming. Hm?"

Now Machal said to his muse with a bow: "Excuse me please – " and returned reluctantly from the opaline world; the misunderstanding was simply too much. "No," he insisted, "it means I'm too sad right now. It means that now is the time when Nature misunderstands all that comes into being, it means that I'm tired – tired of all this painful burgeoning."

"I beg your pardon," the novelist tapped him on the shoulder with his fashionably yellow glove, "that may well be, but that's not Spring."

And the painter thought: no, that's not Spring.

"In the lovely month of May," declaimed the actor.

"Once," breathed the poet, motioning with his hand to push back this "once" still further, "once it may have been as we find it in old poems – Spring: 'light and love and life'. Anyone who believes that now is lying to himself." He heaved a sigh.

What a pity, thought the painter, no more Spring, then.

8

But Machal lifted his face, disfigured by huge freckles, up into the clear afternoon light; out the window he could just barely see the ramp of the National Theater[4], next to which a policeman paced back and forth. That was not exactly what he wanted to show them, but all the same he said:

"Just look outside. This struggle against the foolish fallow clods which every fine, weak seed must fight to come by its summer. Here," and he lifted himself up a few notches – "the helpless flower stands yearning to bloom; that is all it can do, it doesn't mean to bother a soul, and yet everyone is against it: the black soil which lets it past only after long pleas, and the days which scatter warmth and rain and wind down willy-nilly, and the nights which creep up slowly to throttle it with icy fingers. This cowardly sad struggle, that is Spring." Machal shivered; his eyes died. "King Bohusch" stared at him. That was a very unfair thing the poet had said, it seemed to him, and many objections rose to mind. He felt moved to stand up towering and serene to defend the Spring, which was full of sun and triumph all the same. So many fine thoughts rose to his head that his cheeks grew warm and for a moment he forgot to breathe.

---

[4] National Theater: Theater dedicated in 1881 and reopened after a fire in 1883. The National Theater is one of the greatest symbols of the so-called Czech national renaissance. The building, which holds more than 1800 spectators, was built with only domestic materials according to a design by the architect Josef Zítek and decorated by the leading artists of the time ("the generation of the National Theater"). It is one of Prague's most splendid Renaissance revival structures.

But, oh, what good would it do to rise; they would hardly have noticed, for sitting on the high velvet seat Bohusch almost seemed taller than when he stood. And his voice would have flown scarcely as far as Norinski; at such ranges it grew unsure and flailed like a wounded bird. Bohusch knew that. And so he was silent, pressed together his lips, which seemed as if carved of wood, and began quietly, as so often in childhood, to play by himself with all those golden thoughts, building whole mountains and castles from whose slender pillared windows his dreams greeted him. And so rich was he that he could build new palaces every time, none resembling any of the old ones, which is saying quite a bit, for the little man had passed the time like this for more than thirty years, since perhaps the age of five – and yet had never repeated himself. Now (Machal probably felt he was sitting in his absinthe glass again) the others were talking pell-mell of loud things and everyday matters, and over it all the actor's bass voice hovered with outspread wings. But Bohusch worked away on his apologia of Spring in the corner. Really he only knew it as it looked in the dark damp Hirschgraben[5] or in the Malvasinka Cemetery[6]; once, as a child, he had seen it in the wild

---

[5] Hirschgraben (lit. stag trench): Cleft in the hillside along the north wall of the Prague Castle where game was hunted in earlier centuries.

[6] Malvasinka (Czech *Malvazinka*): Cemetery in the Prague district of Smíchov with some notable gravestones, named after a previous owner of the property.

Schárka[7], and even now he still heard an old faint echo of that sunny day in his breast. Then what a joy it must be to behold out there where its home is, far from the city and its turmoil, and it irked him that the people about him, people who had seen the world, allowed the Spring to be repudiated. He had to tell them that. But his lips' timid foray quickly went under in the general repartee, leaving not a trace, and poor Bohusch could think of nothing else to say. As if in fear of betrayal his thoughts fled the fine assembly in anxious haste; in their place a single idea filled his mind, and he spoke it will-less and unnoticed: Yes, my father. It was a moment before the hunchback realized why he had thought of him now. He saw him: in his enormous, dark-blue, gold-braided fur coat whose collar seemed to merge with his mighty beard, he paced back and forth in the lofty, light-drenched hall of the old princely palace on Spornergasse[8] with long, self-confident strides. The golden knob of his staff almost touched the golden fringe on the brim of his three-cornered hat, beneath which his eyes were grave and vigilant. Then the sickly little Bohusch would often stand behind the door of the porter's apartment, shyly peering through

[7] Schárka (Czech *Žárka*): Valley on the western edge of Prague through which the Žárka brook flows.

[8] Spornergasse: At the time a common nickname for Nerudova Street in the Lesser Quarter. One explanation for the nickname is that, due to the steepness of the street, rafters ("Sporen") were laid across to provide more traction for the vehicles. The birthplace of the Czech writer Jan Neruda is located on Nerudova Street, as are a number of imposing palaces.

11

a crack to watch his father's mighty strides. His figure was taller than anyone's, even towering above the old prince, before whom he would doff his gold-braided hat deeply without much of a bow. As far back as Bohusch looked, he could recall not a single kiss or a smile from this man, but his figure and his voice were among the most vivid impressions of his impoverished childhood. And that was why he always thought of his father in envying the long-dead man these two attributes, saying to himself: Really both are as good as unused now; he no longer needs either figure or voice, so why has he taken it all with him? And when the hunchback thought that, the same thing always happened: all at once he felt something pick him up, carry him off. His thoughts were no longer within him, they ran ahead of him, and he had to give chase to capture them again. You couldn't just let them run off like that. Each time he caught up with them at the same place, breathless. It was a bright fall night with hasty clouds. The fleeting light was just patient enough to show Bohusch a marble slab on which was written, half-hidden by wild branches: Vitězlav Bohusch, princely porter. And every time the little man read that, he began to dig in the grass and the clods with greedy nails until he grew weaker and weaker and the breath of the moist earth grew heavier and danker and at last his bloody nails shrieked on the smooth wood of a big yellow coffin. And then he saw himself kneeling on the box in the black pit, at a loss for a second or two. Until the solution came to him, the same one every time: It should be possible to put his head through this plank like a window-pane. Hadn't he always been made fun of for his thick skull? Well, it had to be good for something, right? Crash! The plank gives way – of course – like a window-pane, and reaching out his hand Bohusch takes his father's chest from the musty darkness and buckles it about his shy shoulders like a suit of armor, and he reaches in again and seeks and seeks with spasmodic fingers and sends his other hand to help and cannot comprehend that with both sore hands he is unable to find his father's voice.

In the evenings of the early spring the air has a moist coolness which settles softly on all colors and makes them lighter and more alike. Almost all the pale houses on the quay have taken on the faint color of the sky, and only their windows flare now and then in hot brilliance, fading appeased into the twilight as soon as the sun ceases to disturb them. Then only the tower of St. Vitus[9] still stands there

[9] St. Vitus: Even before the turn of the first millenium the rotunda which occupied the site of the present St. Vitus Cathedral had a certain importance, as it housed an arm of the Auxiliary Saint Vitus, a Sicilian martyr from the 4th century A. D.. In the 11th century a three-bayed basilica replaced the rotunda, soon becoming the church in which the Přemyslids were crowned and buried. In 1344 Charles IV entrusted the French architect Mathieu d'Arras with the construction of a Gothic cathedral. After the death of the architect the Swabian Peter Parler carried on with the construction. However, the course of events, in particular the Hussite Wars which began in 1419, prevented the cathedral from being completed until the 20th century. St. Vitus is the episcopal cathedral of the Archbishopric of Prague.

upright in its eternal aged grey. "It really is a landmark," Bohusch said to the taciturn student. "It outstays every twilight and is always just the same. In the color, I mean. Don't you think?"

Rezek had not heard a thing. He gazed across at the bridge tower on the Lesser Quarter side, where the lamps were just being lit.

Bohusch went on: "I know my little mother Prague down to the heart of her – to the heart of her," he repeated, as if someone had doubted his assertion, "for that must be her heart, after all, the Lesser Quarter with the Hradschin[10]. The heart always holds what's most secret, and you see, there is so much that is secret in these old houses. I have to tell you, Rezek, since you're from the country and maybe you don't know it yet. But there are old chapels there, Jesus, and what strange things there are inside. Pictures and hanging lamps, and whole chests, Rezek, I'm not lying, whole chests full of

[10] Lesser Quarter with the Hradschin: The castle ("Hradschin" in German, "Hradčany" in Czech) and the entire citadel (Hradčany) lies on the left bank of the Vltava on a long hill, a rocky ridge rising above the Lesser Quarter. Hrad means "castle" in Czech, and thus the entire district derives its name from the venerable Prague Castle. The most influential Bohemian families such as the Czernins, the Lobkowitzes, the Dietrichsteins, the Martinitzes, the Rosenbergs and the Schwarzenbergs also settled in the citadel in the immediate vicinity of the king. By the 17th century, when land for building grew scarce around the castle, the nobility began to build in the Lesser Quarter below the castle. The historical Prague districts of the Lesser Quarter and the Hradschin, on the left bank of the Vltava, and the Old Town and the New Town on the right bank, were incorporated in 1784 as one of Joseph II's administrative reforms.

14

gold. And from these old chapels passageways go far, far beneath the entire city, maybe all the way to Vienna."

Rezek looked at the cripple sidelong.

"By my soul," swore Bohusch, putting his hand to his thick, crooked chest. "I wouldn't have believed it either. Never, not upon my life. But one time I saw it, not in a chapel, but – "

"Where?" the student probed suddenly with such sharp interest that the little man gave a start.

"You see," he said, "you don't believe it. But in our cellar there's a hollow at the very end, about two steps down, and then a hole in the wall, just big enough for someone to crawl through – like that – on all fours, of course." Bohusch laughed his broken laugh.

"Well –" Rezek urged, then went on more calmly, shaping a cigarette with his animated fingers, "what then?"

"I never would have crawled in there. God forbid. But one time the candle I'd brought down with me fell into the old firewood, still burning. My horror! Well, you can picture it, Rezek, a burning candle in old, dry wood. At last I find it, it had gone out, of course, but in sheer panic I go on digging. There could have been a spark down in there somewhere. Suddenly I slide down deeper on top of the wood and I'm sitting in front of the hole. I look inside. Not possible. Another cellar, I think. I shine the light in. But it's just a passageway, going God knows how far, God knows."

They were walking very slowly down the quay

now, toward the stone bridge[11]. Rezek took a long pull on his thoroughly damp cigarette and said without looking down at Bohusch: "Of course, I suppose it's long since been walled up, that hole?"

"Walled up?" tittered Bohusch, "Walled up," beside himself with mirth, "Who would wall up a thing like that?"

"Well, you must have reported it, at least?" The student looked exasperated. His dark eyes crouched in his pale face as if to pounce on the little man's answer.

He had only just taken a hold of himself again: "My mother, you know – I told her. And she said: 'A hole? What business is that of ours? Stack the wood back in front of it the way it was.' And so I stacked the wood in front of it the way it was." The student nodded distractedly and then said quickly: "It's cold for April." He hunched his angular shoulders and pulled together the front of the shabby yellow summer overcoat which he had worn all winter: "Shall we duck into that cafe over there? A *Tschaj* will do us good. Come on." He thrust his hand under the hunchback's arm and tried to drag him along. Bohusch balked: "Now, now, Rezek, as if we hadn't been sitting in the cafe long enough." "Yes, with *them*." The student filled the last word with contempt. "I want to chat with *you*, Bohusch, not with those fine gentlemen, those artists." "What are you saying?"

---

[11] Stone bridge: old name for the Charles Bridge, built in 1357, which connects the Old Town and the Lesser Quarter.

goggled Bohusch. "Our people must be proud of them." Rezek stopped where he was, very pale: "If only those gentlemen were proud of the people. But believe me, they're completely unaware of each other – the people of them and they of the people. I ask you, what are they, are those Czechs, well? Just look at one of them, any one. Karás writes about our art for German papers. And our art, what is that? Perhaps songs that could be sung by this very young, healthy, barely-awoken people? Tales of its strength and its courage and its freedom? Pictures of its homeland? Well? Not a trace. These gentlemen don't know a thing about *that*. They aren't of this day, unlike our people which is still so childish, full of wishes and without a single fulfillment. They've become finished things overnight. Over-ripe. After all, that's much more convenient than going your own long way through oppression as the people must, our poor people! It's nearly effortless. You import everything from Paris: your clothes and your convictions, thoughts and inspiration. Yesterday you were a child and today you're a young dotard, over-sated. You know everything all of a sudden, and you make it into art. You paint orgies and atrocities. You seek the whore in the woman and extol her in novels; then you condemn this whore in naughty songs and celebrate love between men in turgid stanzas, and at last you've reached your goal: you no longer extol, and you no longer condemn either. You're tired of it. You're beyond all that anyway. You're a mystic. You aren't even at home here anymore, in Bohemia, the very idea! Your homeland is somewhere – I don't know – at the source of Life Itself. That's a lark, isn't it? Just as our people stirs and feels for the first time how young and healthy it is, and the new timid strength of the beginning courses through its veins, the artists desecrate its language by using its Spring for the sick art of an end." The student had talked himself hot and hoarse. They were still standing in the same place. Passers-by were beginning to stare, and a policeman shot them suspicious looks from time to time. Bohusch looked up at the student silently, and he seemed to loom in the night as tall and proud as the old cathedral spire on the other bank. –

Now Rezek said in a different voice, irritated by the people's curiosity: "Come on, let's go to the cafe."

And Bohusch went with him, completely under the spell of the command. It did not cross his mind to say no. But when they stopped at the door of the little cafe he said timidly, "I really can't, Mr. Rezek, forgive me, but really I can't now. My mother, you know. She expects me home in the evening. And she'd worry if I didn't come. That's her way. I'm sorry..."

The student interrupted him curtly: "Then I'll walk you home." And they walked to the Lesser Quarter. In silence. As they passed the policeman the cripple felt him give Rezek a dark, suspicious look. He glanced up; but the student had already turned his head away and spat indifferently in the other direction, apparently aiming at the corner-stone. Bohusch reflected: he felt a kinship between the fine thoughts which had come to him that afternoon in the "National" and what Rezek had said and was going to say now. It was the first time he had had this feeling, though he often encountered the student; he had always taken him for a fool. Why? Because he was usually so quiet? But for the very same reason people probably thought that he, Bohusch, was slow-witted. Yet how beautiful the student's face, in itself gaunt and ugly, had become during his fervent words. All that was angular and wooden in his face and his gestures took on a touch of sublimity, becoming stern, imperious, ruthless. This rangy young man who had grown too fast, been fed too poorly and clothed too shabbily had quite unexpectedly assumed something elemental, eternal in Bohusch's eyes, and as he walked along at his side he could not escape the feeling that he should mark this day: Saturday, the 17th of April. This notion grew within him, firm and distinct, but in the background of his soul, as it were, while at the front his own Self stood up, bowed, and said to Bohusch: I won't stand for that, decidedly not! My dear fellow, you have no right to hide all the treasures I give you – you, Bohusch. Out with it. Speak. Let the people know I'm rich. I know what you're going to say. You're ugly. But just speak first. Speech beautifies. As you just saw. Promise me. – And poor Bohusch gave his Self his word of honor: By all means, from now on I will speak. And Bohusch was about to begin when the student came to a stop beside him and pointed across the Vltava, on whose high dark waves lost lights drifted. "Look there, the Vyschehrad[12], Libuše's old ancestral castle, and the Hradschin there, and the Church of Our Lady of the Týn[13] behind us, shrines all of them. If the gentlemen must flee into the past, as they're always claiming, why not into *this* past? Why do they tell us about the Orient and the Crusades and the dark Middle Ages? That's an artistic question, they say. No, I say: That is a question of the heart. It's no coincidence that they "respond" to those remote things while what is close and familiar means nothing to them. They're simply strangers. And our people anxiously tends its old, helpless traditions, which for all its care grow paler and paler from grandchild to grandchild, until at last it barely knows of the living riches of its homeland. Of course! It would be too demeaning for those fine gentlemen to accompany our people to its holy heirlooms and tell it in new clear words of their ancient worth and their sacred dignity."

[12] Vyschehrad: German spelling of Czech *Vyšehrad* (= high castle): The Vyšehrad is a castle complex in the south of Prague, surrounded by myths and legends; it is supposed to have been the residence of the legendary Princess Libuše.

[13] Church of Our Lady of the Týn (Czech *Týnský chrám*): The Church of Our Lady of the Týn in the Old Town was so named because of its proximity to the "Týn Yard", a fortified ("týn" means "fortification") area of the city in which the chiefly German merchants offered their wares. The church was endowed by German merchants in the mid-14th century. The construction was supervised by Peter Parler's workshop. To this day the 80-meter towers, each with eight pointed side towers, have remained a characteristic point of reference amidst Prague's labyrinth of roofs.

Bohusch stared at the stones of the sidewalk and said quietly, as if forcing himself, interrupted again and again by hemming and hawing:

"You're right, Rezek, you're quite definitely right. I don't understand all that very well, what you're saying there isn't so simple, by no means. But you're right. I've thought that myself sometimes. Why do they paint this and not that. Why do they write this way and not that way... but if you don't mind my saying so, if the writers don't write about the Hradschin and the Teyn, it doesn't matter, it doesn't matter. I mean – you see, I know my little mother Prague down to the heart of her, yes, and no writer has ever told me anything about that. You only need to grow up amidst these churches and palaces. God knows they don't need anyone to speak for them, they speak themselves, I say. If only you can hear them. Oh, the stories they know. My friend, I'll tell you a few some day. Or better: You should hear my mother on the subject."

Rezek made an impatient movement. Bohusch noticed it at once and hesitated for a moment, then: "Forgive me. All I wanted to say is really... yes, well, it's not so bad about the Hradschin, but the other things. That aren't the past. The alley there and these people and more than anything the fields outside the city and the people there. You must have seen that too: A field, you know, a field with no end, sad and grey. And behind it the evening. And nothing, only a few trees and a few people; and the trees stooped and the people too. Or a quarry, the kind out there past Smichov[14]. The little pebbles roll down the bald grey mountain into the skip. How that sounds. Yes, that's a song too; and down there men sit cutting the grey stones all day, making them into fine smooth little cubes and seeing the sun dimly through the horn glasses over their eyes. And sometimes the younger ones forget and start to sing softly, not a rowdy song, God forbid, something that fits the rhythm, *"Kde domov můj"*[15] or the like. And then everyone listens. But it doesn't last long. Soon the boy remembers how harsh the stone dust is, bad for the lungs, and then, well, he's quiet again... But – you must forgive me –" the little man looked about helplessly, but took heart again when he saw that the student's eyes were on him, serious and attentive. He felt this to be a triumph, and he continued his speech with more confidence than before: "All I wanted to say is: Why don't they paint that, why? Why don't they write something like that? That's Czech, after all – it's so sad."

Rezek only nodded and said: "Do you think our people is very sad?"

Bohusch pondered: "Of course," he admitted hesitantly, "I know so little really, I don't get about much. But I think so."

[14] Smichov: German spelling of Czech *Smíchov*; once secluded suburb of Prague (with the summer residence Bertramka), since the 19th century a traditional working-class neighborhood.

[15] *Kde domov můj*: Beginning of a poem by Josef Kajetán Tyl (1834), meaning, "Where my homeland is"; since 1918 national anthem of Czechoslovakia and, today, the Czech Republic.

"Why?"

"Why, you ask? God, should I know that? The parents are sad, and the children are too, and they stay that way. As soon as they can walk they see sad Nepomuk[16] outside the door holding the crucified Jesus in his arms, and the old willow by the village pond, and the sunflowers in the little garden which tire so early in the quiet sun. Does that make people happy? And then they learn hatred so early on. The Germans are everywhere, and we must hate the Germans. I ask you, what's the good of that? Hatred makes people so unhappy. Let the Germans do as they please. They don't understand our land, anyway, and that's why they'll never be able to take it away from us. On the borders there are big forests and mountains where the Germans sit tight, aren't there? But really they only frame the land. Everything in between, all the fields and meadows and rivers, that's our homeland, that belongs to us as we belong to it with everything in us."

"As slaves" – Rezek put in contemptuously.

"Don't say that. Please. Not as slaves. As children. Maybe not as fully recognized children, not with a full right of inheritance – at this time. But still as true, natural children. You must feel that. You yourself said: our people is young and healthy. Well then, it must be strong, too, and it won't surrender. Maybe here and there someone is in chains – today. That

---

[16] Nepomuk: John of Nepomuk (1350-1393), Bohemian saint and martyr who was drowned in the Vltava at the command of King Wenceslas IV.

will pass. I know, someone's written "Slave Songs"[17], one of the older ones. He is wrong. No upright man of our people makes noise with his chains. Surely not. He even holds them up carefully as he walks so that the dear earth knows nothing of his misery... Those are the upright ones among us."

Now they had just reached the beginning of the Brückengasse[18]; they squeezed through the thicker crowds of pedestrians and quickly turned into the next narrow side-alley. In the light of the next lantern the student regarded his companion with undisguised astonishment; he shook his head, seemed to crush something on his lips and said: "You're an orator, Bohusch."

"Oh," went the little man, looking completely overwhelmed.

"No, seriously. Only you have to be told so. That part about the Germans... If you keep your wits about you, the people may need you some day."

"Whaaat?" went Bohusch, and nearly burst out laughing in alarm and discomfiture. But Rezek's lips were pressed together tightly; he was silent and looked deadly earnest. At that

---

[17] "Slave Songs": In 1894 (German edition 1897) the Czech poet Svatopluk Čech (1846-1908) published political poems entitled "Songs of a Slave" *("Písně otroka")* in which he assumes the persona of a wrathful, reproachful Old Testament prophet who returns from his cave in the mountains to find nothing but slavery, obsequiousness and baseness, and breaks his staff over his dearly-beloved nation.

[18] Brückengasse (Czech *Mostecká*, meaning "Bridge Street"): street connecting the Charles Bridge to the Lesser Quarter Square, the central square of the Lesser Quarter.

the hunchback felt very afraid. He drew closer to the student and whispered:

"That's just the way I think about it. Really. I don't know. Maybe it's not like that. I can't really say. You mustn't think badly of me, Mr. Rezek." And all at once he was utterly dejected. "You see, I'm such a poor devil. If only you knew how poor I am. In the morning I copy out papers in the office, and the evening I spend with my mother, she's so old and hardly sees a thing anymore. It's like that every day. And on Sunday when I see my Františka, do you know where we pass the time then? In the Malvasinka. Where the green crosses stand, one just like the other. All those children buried there, and there's nothing but a Christian name on the little metal plates, 'little Karel' or 'little Marie', and a prayer. That's how it is there. And that's where we spend our Sundays. 'Here we're alone, *milatschku*[19]', says my Frantischka. 'Yes,' I say, 'Frantischka, we're alone here.' Though I know we're surrounded by dead people. Does that matter? There's always something in between, sometimes spring, sometimes snow. – Oh, I'm such a poor devil."

"Now, now," soothed Rezek; they were already standing in front of the house where Bohusch shared two attic rooms with his old mother. The student was evidently in a hurry. "You aren't angry with me, are you, Mr. Rezek," pleaded the hunchback. "There's no cause for that,"

[19] "milatschku": German spelling of Czech *miláčku*: (vocative of *miláček* = beloved).

Rezek replied hastily. "Good night. I suppose I'll see you tomorrow in the cafe!"

"Yes, tomorrow, maybe – although, it's Sunday, my Frantischka and I are – yes – good night."

Rezek, who had already gone a few steps, suddenly came back. He laid his nervous hand on the little man's shoulder and added very quickly, without particular emphasis:

"Really, you've made me quite curious, Bohusch, you have. How would you like to show me into the cellar some time?"...

"Cellar?"

"Oh, you know, that hole."

"Oh yes, if you like, of course."

"Good, soon then, when?..."

"Whenever you like."

"Tomorrow morning?"

"Tomorrow morning."

And they agreed upon the time. –

No one noticed Bohusch show a guest into the cellar of the gloomy old house on Hieronymous-Gasse Sunday morning. The two descended as cautiously as if to avoid waking a sleeper; they cleared aside the wood below, and then the stranger, a very taciturn fellow, crawled into the secret passageway with the lantern. The hunchback stood staring after him. For a while the hole was bright, then the streaks of light faded at the edges, and finally a few reflections fluttered back and forth in the black frame, wounded their wings against the walls and fell dead in the boundless dark. Bohusch listened.

Steps echoed far away, further and further. All at once he was afraid. He thought: Why is he doing this? At last he no longer heard the steps, and now he began to call. His words had a strange sound; they carried the beating of his heart, which he felt in his throat, growing wilder and more frantic: "Be careful, Rezek! – Rezek, don't go any further. What are you doing? Now, now. You mustn't go any further. Here, here. Do you hear? Jesus Mary, where are you? No foolishness; you never know..." Suddenly the light of the lantern struck him full on, so startlingly that the little man still evinced all the signs of fear and alarm for some time, cutting a comical figure in his breathless confusion. With a single leap Rezek was beside him, but seemed not to notice him at all. A certain satisfaction flared up in his dark eyes, fading quickly, and that stern reserve came over his face, turning every line of it to stone. "Well?" Bohusch finally managed to say, taking the lantern from the other's hand to have the light nice and close and safe. All at once the student struck him as awfully simple, even a bit comical, and when he realized that in his panic he had been shouting in the wrong direction the whole time, where there was no hole, his apprehension melted away, it seemed to spill off his body in hollow, uncontrollable laughter. Now he was in the mood to find everything funny, and it seemed an exquisite joke that the gaunt student was stacking the wood up in front of the secret door again and acting so solemn and important. As they climbed the stairs he invited Rezek to come up and visit after all. His mother was sure to be home, and he would not regret taking the time to hear wonderful stories and perhaps drink a glass of Gilka (yes, he had such delicacies, the poor Bohusch!).The student excused himself tersely. He had urgent obligations and would come another time. Incidentally, it had been quite interesting down there – many thanks. Bohusch was keenly disappointed; he would so have liked to chat right now. But Rezek was not to be moved. He bade a curt farewell; as he left he heard the hunchback call a very loud "good morning" to someone on the second floor as he waddled overeagerly up the stairs. The student strode hastily up the Brückengasse. He stood out as a very busy person will stand out among idlers, and his slender black figure seemed to clamber its way along these slow bright Sunday strollers who streamed toward the Church of St. Nicholas[20].

Not much later the wretched figure of "King Bohusch" appeared in the festive crowd. In this neighborhood most people knew him, knew the nickname which, God knows why, he had borne since his schooldays, and cocky boys giggled and shouted "King Bohusch" behind his back, which was so much rounder and uglier under his black Sunday coat. Not letting this bother

[20] Church of St. Nicholas: The Church of St. Nicholas on the Lesser Quarter Square (not to be confused with the Church of St. Nicholas on the Old Quarter Square) is the gem of the Dientzenhofer family of architects, one of the most beautiful examples of Baroque church architecture in Bohemia.

him, the cripple drifted with the crowd for a while, then turned and walked toward the Old Town, smiling the whole time. He wanted to meet someone; he felt like declaring to someone that though life may have its rough edges, on the whole it is a splendid thing, that the Czechs are a proud and patriotic people and Prague a city – ("just look this Rudolfinum[21], if you please" – he would have said now) – a city whose equal you wouldn't find next door. The best chance of finding someone was on Ferdinandstrasse[22] and "am Graben"[23], on whose broad sidewalks all modern Prague spends its Sunday noon, and he steered in that direction in the hope of seeing someone or other – even Machal or Pátek. Hardly had he thought this when he saw Pátek. The smart novelist was walking along just in front of him. He wore a

[21] Rudolfinum: The concert hall, also called "artists' house" (Dům umělců), was named after the Crown Prince of the Habsburg Throne, Archduke Rudolf, who died tragically in Mayerling in 1889. The Rudolfinum, built by the Prague architects Josef Schulz (National Museum) and Josef Zítek (National Theater), is one of the city's most distinguished Renaissance revival buildings.

[22] Ferdinandstrasse: National Street (Czech: Národní třída) was called Ferdinandstrasse until 1918 in memory of Emperor Ferdinand V., who had lived in the Prague castle after abdicating in 1848. It separates the Old Town, including the houses on the north side of the street, from the New Town in the south. While the Graben was mainly the promenade of the Prague Germans, National Street was soon the fashionable boulevard of the Czechs.

[23] Am Graben (Czech Na příkopě): The present-day shopping street and promenade between the Magazine and Wenceslas Square derives its name (meaning "on the moat") from the moat which ran down its middle until 1816, dividing the Old Town from the New Town.

brand-new light-grey suit, to show his support of the rather timid spring, as it were, and the sharp crease of his trousers, never breaking in his stride, reached impeccably to his shining patent-leather shoes, which he gracefully displayed to best advantage. When Bohusch overtook and addressed him, he raised his gloved hand (café au lait, 6¾) casually to the brim of his low top-hat, showing little willingness to be drawn into a conversation. But Bohusch was so happy to find someone that he forgot his shyness and simply came along without waiting to be invited. And now and then Pátek would toss down some phrase; that is, he would drop it, little caring whether or not the little man caught the precious fragments. The other, though, spoke incessantly, now and then unwinding in his loud laughter. Everything was grist to his mill. His jokes, not always entirely felicitous, attracted attention and displeasure right and left, and the elegant young man, dispensing greetings on all sides, felt distinctly uncomfortable in the company of this "proletarian gone wrong", as he liked to call Bohusch. At the next corner he pretended to notice a good friend on the other side of the street; he peered across for a while, murmured something unintelligible and skipped off before Bohusch realized what was going on. The hunchback went on, stopped again ten steps later, sought the figure of the fugitive in the throng on the other side, and saw that Pátek was walking by himself. At that the laughter faded from his broad face; he cursed at someone who had just brushed him in passing, turned about and with ruthless shoulders bored his way to a side alley where there was no sun and no people. Tears were in his eyes. – For a while he thought of visiting Schileder in his studio. He was always tolerated there. Even if the painter was busy, he was allowed to slink off into a soft corner of the big room with some portfolio or other, looking at pictures for hours and letting his eyes wander along the high ledges where the most incongruous things, the most fabulous devices stood companionably, thickly veiled by years of dust. He had often sat there for hours unnoticed, and whenever he had discovered a piece of velvet or colorful wrinkled, shimmering silk he would not let the rag out of his sight, and the painter would always give it to him. Then he would storm up his four flights of stairs wild with impatience to step in front of the mirror, dressed up with the piece of cloth. Yes, poor Bohusch saw his black coat, too old in any case, as inferior, unworthy Sunday dress, and even as a child he had dreamed of showing himself to the world in splendid and unconventional clothes. In his school days he had served as an altar boy at High Mass just to wear the red surplice, and later he fervently desired to become a solider for the sake of the showy uniform. All that was water under the bridge, and now he could never hope to wear anything but this shabby black coat, even on the most festive occasion, unless Frantischka decided to marry him after all; for those festivities he would not hesitate to have a new one made, and it would have to have a wide velvet collar. His father's embroidered vest was also waiting for that day; Bohusch was going to have it tailored to fit him then – but only when the time came. Not to spend the money in vain. And would the time ever come?... Last Sunday Bohusch had waited for his beloved in vain. What if she stayed away again today?

In the poorer cemeteries, where no gardener's hand adorns mighty marble monuments with calculating art, it is thus: Spring, in his innocence, steps inside, and the creaking of the rusty gate is the last noise he hears. He has no idea where he is. But he likes it here in these quiet walls behind which life surges far away, among these little angels of gleaming earthenware who have folded their hands to pray to him. To whom else? Nor is there is any better stay for the fearful young bindweed than a cross on which, once it has reached that high, it can stretch out to the left or the right as far as it wants, as if in reward. And, thus indulged, Spring grows up faster in such a place than elsewhere. At any rate, the dark little figure of Bohusch was almost lost in the tumult of primulas and anemones, and above him the wind crouched in a tree which had flowers before its leaves came, now and then tossing a flower into his lap and waving the dainty twigs as roguishly as if to deluge the lonely man any moment. But the hunchback was not in the mood to take its meaning. He brushed the flowers sullenly from his black sleeves and gazed past the sunny Sunday at another day, another day altogether. That was in a cemetery too. About three years ago. A few people dressed in black stood around the open grave: the men with a certain air of cavalier-like distinction, with great beards or smooth-shaved faces, wearing those furrows about the lips which according to general agreement indicate sorrow and emotion, the women, much more insignificant, with handkerchiefs in their hands, and at the center of this solemn group a small, helpless, white-haired woman. She was completely overwhelmed by her pain; it had taken total possession of her. Every twitch of her pitiful figure, every plea of her choked voice belonged to it. It had made her forget everything around her, even her son, poor Bohusch. He was cruelly surprised. He had never seen his mother like this before. He himself felt nothing out of the ordinary. He only wondered how his father could have found room in the coffin. The box did not look especially large; he must be lying like *this*. Here he pictured his father with his knees drawn up a bit, and he reflected that if the dead man ever got the unheard-of notion into his head to stretch out his legs, the yellow box would surely give way, top or bottom. Filled with thoughts of this kind, he waited calmly for the party to head back. But with his ceaselessly sobbing old mother unable to recognize him in her pain, he grew deeply alarmed. He did not understand that for fear of her husband, who could not bear scenes, the poor little woman had never dared to weep in all the forty years of her marriage, except perhaps for the first two, and now was unconsciously weeping away all she had neglected, one year after the other, in the redeeming pleasure of a certain liberation. And forty years can't be wept away in the wink of an eye. Bohusch looked helplessly from one person to the other. All of them went past him, the dead man's friends and comrades, and the most tactful among them squeezed his hand silently, while the eyes of the accompanying women spilled over every time, and the princely valet said in the correct German of the foreigner: "He was not even so old, your father." That was meant to emphasize that the deceased porter had been two years older than himself, His Highness's English valet. Each handshake made Bohusch more anxious; he realized that something out of the ordinary must have happened, and, alarmed by the people's stiff solemnity, he lagged several paces behind the procession. Suddenly he felt two arms reach down to him, and when he looked up, a young blonde lady had just kissed him on the forehead. She had cool lips, he felt that, and what he liked even better: she wasn't weeping. She just had very, very sad eyes. But when the hunchback met her gaze, he thought of a dark forest. Nothing frightening, just a dark forest, which is habitable, after all. And so he liked the sad eyes immediately, the sad eyes of his Frantischka. – As a matter of fact: no one knew the lady then, no one in the funeral party knew her name; she had simply come along. Two old beggar women stood at the cemetery gate, rosaries in their withered hands.

They were in the middle of their seventeenth "Ave..."; as Bohusch came past with his new friend, hand in hand; they interrupted their prayers, and one said with a grin: "That girl there with the hunchback, she was the darling of the late lamented." And by and by their hissing chuckles turned into the eighteenth "Ave". But Bohusch had not heard that. – He saw the blonde girl again, and one time when she caressed his forehead with her hand and said: "You're such a good, good fellow," he kissed that hand, and his heart raced. He felt an ice-cold shiver run down his back, everything collapsed in his head with a crash, he squeezed his hands together until he could have cried out in pain, and instead of crying out he whispered: "You're my darling, aren't you?" And at that she laughed, laughed loud and nodded, and her eyes were full of that dear sadness. But that was long ago now, and Bohusch, sitting under the blossoming tree in the Malvasinka, would have dearly liked to ask Frantischka that again. Instead he stared at the evening's red face and knew: now she'll never come. There was not the slightest hope in him; all the same he went on sitting there among the mounds and crosses, enthralled by the dark desire to dwell here with the same right as all his neighbors. What would he have to do? God, his eyes would simply have to let go of those towers there, that gently dissolving slope, take leave of the sky, of the first evening star, and something deep within him would have to draw breath once again, say "Frantischka" and then nothing

more. That would be all, and is that so hard? –
It must have been hard, for Bohusch rose and
went down the rutted path and along the broad
main street. There a glimmering grey fog
seeped down, seeming to hold the gas flames
captive in the air so that they scattered none of
their light on the thick crowds of tired tourists
who took eerie form out of the immensity just
two steps ahead of the lonely man and sank
back abruptly into the void behind him. And if
Bohusch, following his innermost instinct, had
kept walking without looking up, he would
surely have landed in the Vltava, still turbulent with drifting ice, just as a weary nag finds
its way into the quiet stall – without looking
up. But Bohusch *looked up*. The fog around
him began to speak to him in mighty, swelling
tones, and all the towers to which he had meant
to bid farewell raised their solemn Ave-voices.
It was as if some great festivities were being
held up there over the roofs, behind the impen-
etrable dank folds, and the cripple's soul was
suddenly aloft, and before he could stop it, it
rose up in the mystical jubilation of the air.
And poor Bohusch stood there gazing after it. –
He remembered that Easter Sunday was in
eight days, and this filled him with such joy
that he came back to his old mother beaming,
and all evening he told such funny stories that
the old women was in a whirl and weak with
laughter. What did it matter that later Bohusch dreamed he and Frantischka were to
marry. He saw everything in the finest of detail,
down to the garnet earrings which clung to his

bride's earlobes like drops of blood. And everything went as it should. The wedding ceremony
was in the big domed church of St. Niklas, and
Bohusch recognized the minister at once. Until
then it was all sane and as if in broad daylight.
But all at once it turned very strange. A young,
oh, such a young girl seized the bride kneeling
at the altar next to him, and cried: "I won't let
you have him, I love him so!" She cried it out
loudly, wildly – and that, if you please, in the
great and solemn church of St. Niklas. It was
only natural that the bridegroom – (he really
was wearing a new coat with a dark red velvet
collar, by the way) – should want to take a closer look at this so very young girl who loved him
that much. He recognized Carla, Frantischka's
younger sister, whom he had met before only
briefly, and was very angry at this disturbance.
But as he looked closer he saw that this blonde
child was wearing a nun's habit, and – he felt
such a shock of joy that he started out of his
sleep. Sitting in bed, it was some time before
he got his bearings. Then he figured how long
it would be until Maundy-Thursday, and as it
was only three days, Bohusch smiled and slept
with this smile, dreamless, until morning.

The square in front of the royal castle in
Prague looks very noble despite the shabby
avenue which crosses it. For: it is entirely surrounded by palaces. The one with the mightiest
effect is the old royal castle with the broad
brow and the big white forecourt, behind whose
baroque grille the tireless sentry paces back
and forth. The ancestral home of the princes of

Schwarzenberg and another, rather dull building gaze across as if caught in a perpetual bow, and to the right of the castle, in a rather pompous pose, the freshly-painted palace of the Archbishop watches over the small dwelling houses of the prelates and canons which fawn up to their powerful patron. Only at one corner, next to the castle, where the castle stairs and the steep Spornergasse end, does a gap remain, and deep within it, in splendid panorama, crowded between the Laurence Hill and the Belvedere, lies Prague – this rich, vast epic of architecture. It unfolds before the eyes of the Hradschin, full of light and life, and new, splendid stanzas are always worthily joining the old ones. At the other end of the row of houses which seems bounded on one side by this luminous look-out is a humble one-storied old building which stands there day in, day out with its hands over its eyes, refusing to see the nearby splendor. The children from the whole neighborhood pass its austere silence with a shy shudder, and if ever they ask for tales of this house, they can't sleep all night, or they have hot dreams in which these pale nuns do strange things. Of course, it must give wings to the youthful imagination to hear that the Barnabites who live their mute demise forever in these cruel walls never exchange a word, even among themselves, and may not allow themselves even as much sun as one might find in another's eyes. They must endure their nights, torn by fearful prayers, in the wooden coffins in which at last – not after very long, no doubt – they are lowered into the plot of ground which is said to be at the very heart of the dark walls and to which Spring has surely never found its way. The monastic order of these Barnabas penitents is long since extinct. The crumbling skulls of the last two comrades lie on a stone altar in the forgotten catacombs of Santa Maria della Victoria, enjoying the prayerless repose of decay. But the nuns are much more tenacious in their suffering. About fifteen years ago, when the rusty repose of the door hinges was disturbed for the last time, white-haired neighbors, gossips with questionable memories, claimed that the seven nuns still living had been joined by an eighth – but those were merely groundless suppositions. Yet younger and sharper-witted people had also peered into the carriage which brought the new victim, and they swore it was a young girl of indescribable beauty and nobility, saying that it was a sin to let this wealth of rare comeliness wither away in the most awful of all convents. And they said other things as well; but that was all gossip about what could have brought about this premature farewell to life; great romantic tales were dreamed up, diverse daggers flashed in sundry Bengalese fires, and the most demonic fairytale princes culled a hypothetical existence from these conjectures. Of course all were convinced that some loud and terrible event was behind this renunciation, forgetting, as always, that it could have been some infinitely quiet torment, one of those deep, silent disappointments which give the most sensitive souls the darkly-apprehended certainty that the peaks and abysses of experience are over and now the wide, wide plain will begin with the little hollows and petty hills, so wearying to wander. The lovely weary child came from the high dark princely house on Spornergasse where Bohusch too played his shy boyish games, and the day on which the closed carriage took Princess Aglaja to her lonely new home was a turning point for him as well, the half-grown boy. Actually he could not even remember how the princess looked at that time; he bore her image inside him from the days when her golden laughter fluttered down the solemn halls like a stray swallow, finally, in defiance of the stiff shocked Englishwoman, losing itself in the free expanses of the rustling park. There the two children met quite often, chattering and joking and chasing each other, as children will when they have shaken off a constraint: Aglaja her governess and Bohusch his quiet faithful sadness. Then came years when the porter's son no longer saw the playmate who had now become a lady; thus in his recollection he pushed the day of her renunciation back to the hours of jubilant childhood, the effect being that the brightest day seemed to have been transformed into the deepest night, the richest summer into the most wretched winter day – without transition. He was confronted with an event whose ruthlessness horrified him and whose significance disabused him forever of the notion that the rich and privileged are the allies of a fate which treats only poor devils with hostility and malice. He relinquished a whole bundle of prejudices then, something of a worldview, of a religion was bestowed upon him, germs which could have ripened within him and perhaps out of him too, if he had been braver. But what could have become deeds, growing free and festive from a strong body, became strange florid dreams in the poor hunchback, shy raptures over a smaller and smaller world which was at last nothing but a slender halo about the image of the princess. His helpless gratitude adorned the image until the dear laughing child became a secret wan beloved and the beloved an adored saint who strongly resembled the Virgin Mary and whose sole purpose was to hear Bohusch's rare wishes and patiently assume all the powerful qualities which his tireless imagination ascribed to her. And what an advantage it gave Bohusch over all other believers that his saint, though unattainable to all the world, nevertheless lived and knew of him as a party to her childhood, which she must have taken along with her into the eternal walls as her only jewel. This relationship was not affected in the least when Bohusch began to call Frantischka his beloved, for by then Aglaja's deification had progressed so far that her transfigured form rose high above all petty drives and voluptuous dreams. Bohusch devoted himself to her only once a year, on Maundy-Thursday, when the church of the Barnabite convent is open to all. This small, dark and rather plain church is completely screened off by a wall in back of the high altar, behind which the nuns take part in the official mass. On the day before the Christian Passion Friday – and on this day only – the voices of the nuns seep quietly through the altar wall and sink down upon the few praying people like a distant lament. Then a listening, an anxious holding of the breath, a tremble goes through the little congregation, the priest at the altar stops in the middle of his prayer, the altar boys peer anxiously into the black corners of the room, and the dark pictures on the walls come to life. Then the shrill mass-bell breaks the spell. The pictures on the walls are dead again, the priest bends over the chalice, and the pious shift on their pews, blow their noses loudly and whisper: "It was so faint, are there still eight of them?" and then they shrug and sigh and snort.

This Maundy Thursday was no different. Bohusch knelt at the very front and waited for the call of his saint. He had not forgotten the sound of her voice, and he was always quite sure he recognized her song in the distant choir. He caught it up and teased it out of the whole like a silk thread from faded stuff. He diverted it, so to speak, and let only the rest reach the other listeners. But today he knew from the very first note: she was gone. And however his fear might deny it, he knew: she was gone. And he leaned forward all the way, and his fear prowled and choked the least sound – but he was more and more sure of it: she was gone, and at last in boundless apprehension he reached his hands out, far, far – and listened with all his fingertips... she was gone. And then a cry rang out within him, in the same moment as the mass-bell, only one cry, and then he collapsed on the hard pew like one abandoned by his God.

The painter Schileder was the first to notice a great change in Bohusch. He wondered briefly what could have caused it, but remained completely in the dark. His wife Mathilde was equally at a loss. So they forgot the surprising phenomenon until, one morning shortly after Easter Sunday, Pátek walked into the studio and said: "The impudence." Schileder laid down his brush and palette and contemplated the agitated fellow, who paced up and down without removing his hat. "Good morning, what's the matter?" But the novelist only repeated "The impudence" several times, then stopped and very gingerly made to set his impeccable top hat on a stack of dusty portfolios. First he poked out one gloved index finger, drawing it back as if he had touched a red-hot stove. He balanced the hat back and forth between his palms with touching helplessness and gave the painter a look of reproach: "You've got dust everywhere," he demurred, "one can't even take off one's things." At length he felt safe, took a seat, and explained in quite a muddle that he had just come from the "National"; they had all been gathered there, discussing all kinds of things. "Do you have any cigarettes?" he interrupted himself, not going on until Schileder had satisfied him. So they had been discussing

all kinds of things. And the – well, the "proletarian gone wrong" had joined in the argument
in such a flagrant and forward manner that he,
Pátek had finally felt obliged to give this pre-
sumptuous fellow a lesson once and for all. "Do
you have any cognac?" he asked at this sus-
penseful moment. He tossed back the cognac
and said with a grimace, heaving himself and
moving to the window: "And do you know what
that person dares? He contradicts: Have you
ever heard anything of the kind, he contradicts. Not only that, he insults me. He has the
gall to insult me." "What did he say?" inquired
the painter. "I don't know." Schileder looked at
him with such surprise that he hastily added,
not without embarrassment: "Yes, well, do you
think I have the time to note such nonsense;
that I was ashamed of him, or something. The
fact is – just imagine: he insults me. How could
one not be ashamed of that person!" For moment
longer the genteel novelist appeared fiercely
indignant, but already he was beginning to
show interest in Schileder's work, examining
this and that and with thumb and forefinger
gingerly lifting up various canvas-covered
frames which stood facing the wall. Schileder
took that in good humor and was not surprised
when the young man soon departed in the best
of moods. Pátek was always like that. In a
brief, more or less effective scene he would
address himself to a vexing incident and deal
with it once and for all, "get over it", as he
expressed himself. That did not prevent the
great getter-over from telling the Bohusch

story five more times that morning, in an increasingly advantageous light, so that the fifth version, in the boudoir of a modern operetta singer, gracefully limned a dualistic worldview whose good principle was triumphantly embodied in the sophisticated figure of the storyteller. – And what everyone knew in the end, in part from their own experience, in part from Pátek's disseminations, had a grain of truth:

Bohusch was a changed man. His beloved and his saint had abandoned him. Now he realized that he had given these two figures so much of himself that only a tiny remnant could still be called his own. For a few hours he debated whether to throw this last possession untouched into the Vltava or whether, after all, his capital was sizeable enough to be invested profitably in the great bank of life. In the midst of these deliberations he suddenly remembered a few words which proved to be decisive. On that strange and memorable evening Rezek had said to him: "The people may need you some day." Of course, Rezek had also said, "If you keep your wits about you." And Bohusch would have gladly sworn that he had more wits about him than ever before. He was braver too. He thought many things and said what he thought, whenever remotely relevant, in rather old-fashioned, prolix sentences; on such occasions he was his own most attentive listener. Only quite seldom, as if in forgetfulness, did he turn shy and taciturn; he was afraid of these moments, when the old Bohusch with his quiet golden thoughts stood before him like a ghost and begged him to return to the silent sadness of the old days. But Bohusch remained steadfast. He spent the entire day in the cafe and on the street, sang, whistled and laughed until people turned to stare at him, stood in front of the shop windows without looking at anything but the fitful reflection of his own ugliness, and was like one awaiting something that does not happen every day. Almost instinctively he sought out Rezek. It was as if he must hear from *his* lips what *the* event would be for him. But he could find the student nowhere. He had moved out of his rooms without leaving an address, and in the "National" no one would admit to having seen him. "He's an odd character," Norinski said once. Schileder nodded, but the new Bohusch mocked: "He's stupid," and laughed his old, wretched laughter which no one shared.

That evening the strange thing occurred. Bohusch, who was neglecting his old mother more and more, came home later than usual. He climbed a few stairs, holding up a burning match. His eyes probed the thick darkness of the narrow, twisting corridor. It struck him that the cellar door was slightly ajar; he groped his way over to try it, opened it gingerly and slipped down the familiar cellar steps with rare determination. His form dissolved completely in the dank darkness from which strange distant noises echoed. Groping his way silently along the cold wall, he found that the wood had been pushed aside and saw a shy flicker of light coming from the secret passage; and he felt afraid for the first time. But another, more powerful feeling drew him onward. First he strained to hear the voices close at hand; unable to make out a thing, he squeezed into the opening just far enough to fill the frame without leaning into the room beyond, an involuntary movement whose agility surprised him. The first thing he saw was a big lantern on the floor not far from him, pouring out a rich light which lapped the tiles like a thin spilled liquid. Young men's feet all around the rim of this puddle of light, and in the middle of the circle the feet of a young girl. Here his gaze clung, creeping slowly up a dress of indeterminate color and finding in the gloom two bright lively girlish hands assisting with passionate gestures the words which Bohusch still could not understand. But he understood the hands. Suddenly he realized that these wild hands were shaking at something, that they wanted to overturn some injustice with their sacred young vehemence. And he began to love these hands. He raised his head gently and sought the face which belonged to these beloved hands. His eyes fought a swift and stubborn battle with the jealous shadows, which kept blotting out the barely-discovered features, and triumphed at last. He recognized Carla. And now he persevered, and his astonished and admiring eyes, defying the darkness, refused to leave the young girl's lovely, inspired face; he sucked the words from her lips until they took on a sound of their own for him, the one from his dreams: "I love him so... I love him so...". All that happened in a single moment. And the next minutes brought this: the young girl spoke more and more quietly, like someone retreating further and further; the words which just now had spilled so proud and many-hued from her lips crept naked and aimless into the darkness, ashamed, and her eyes fixed emptily on something down below and slowly flickered out. There was a stir. The eyes of the listeners followed hers, and for a second Bohusch's big staring eyes held them all captive. Only for a second; then horror seized them, they rose up like rebellious slaves, with frantic whispers and savage curses the crowd fled into the depths of the passageway, and the light sprang in Bohusch's face like a yellow cat. At that he woke and trembled.

"Rezek!" he cried.

Rezek leaned over him.

"Bohusch, you dog! Are you spying on us?" he cried shrilly.

Bohusch rolled his eyes, afraid of the student.

"Are you spying?" he bellowed.

"Rezek!" the cripple bellowed still louder out of the depths of his fear. Nothing came to him but this name. At the same time, his position in the narrow gap put him in an agony of discomfort, and he felt himself begin to weep with despair. The student helped him to his feet; immediately he regretted his faintheartedness, remembered his plans, and said in a sorry attempt at superiority: "I know everything." (He meant the two angry girlish hands.) "So you were eavesdropping?" the student threat-

48

ened anew. At that Bohusch ventured, not
without anxiety: "Rezek, but Rezek, don't be
like that – please don't be like that. Aren't I
one of you too, aren't I? I understand it, don't I?
I'm with you – with all my heart I'm with you."
The student regarded him with ruthless keen-
ness, and the cripple was reduced to complete
helplessness in this penetrating, discerning
gaze. He repeated the same thing several times
before the deliverance came to him: "You would
never have found this without me." He meant
the cellar. "I knew you might need it – and
what for," he emphasized with lying slyness.
And the student let himself be deceived. Coming to a quick decision he said: "Your hand!"
and "Silence." With a certain self-assurance
the cripple placed his short fingers in the hand
of the fanatic; his clasp was without confirma-
tion, without emphasis. He knew he had triumphed and began to name his conditions. He
explained at length that he too would speak
down here, among them, for freedom and the
people. Oh, he had important plans. Only Rezek would have to promise him that he could
speak here. "Yes," said the student, and once
again stressed: "Silence!" – Bohusch nodded at
that indifferently and demanded: "So it's set –
I'll speak here?" The other put him off and
pushed him to the door. He had little fear of
this cripple; still less did he hope anything
from him; he was simply a nuisance. When he
had reached the stairs Rezek called him back
once more. He said "Silence" for the third time
and held something at the grinning man. At

first Bohusch was about to reach for it – then he saw: the student's hard cruel hand, and, jutting from the threatening fist, a long, thin, sharp knife, down whose blade the lamplight flowed like faded blood. And try as he might – Bohusch could not find his smile again. He forced a desperate grimace and climbed the steps to his apartment, shivering. And morning was near. –

After that Bohusch no longer slept nights. He waited day and night for Rezek to call him, and he thought of all that he would say then. Many, many things! In his fantasies the finest was mixed with the crudest; *now* it seemed he must tell how to help the poor orphans in the land, but a second later he was convinced he would counsel, command the people down there to storm churches and palaces. Yes, above all the churches! But always, no matter what the speech, he saw himself as the center of this group, as the master who was obeyed blindly and reverently by the lovely Carla and the many strong young men. He saw himself as the long unrecognized one who at last is heard and honored, and he went through the boundlessness of his time – in which night and day had merged into a monotonous grey gloaming – filled with the desire to convert all to this view of his personality. His faithless saint, craven, had sought refuge from his love and his vengeance behind eternal walls; but Frantischka, who would soon hear of his fame from Carla's lips, would be given the chance to obtain his forgiveness. He debated whether to look for her, and in the end, by bits and pieces over two nights and three days, he wrote a letter to the unworthy beloved. His fawning, fastidious court-hand seemed to go wild on these pages. Most of the letters looked like impudent caricatures of the writer; to crown it all they made a show of their foolery with strangely fashioned costumes and caps, each mocking and ridiculing the others behind their backs. In the first part of this sprawling missive he assured her, fully in the spirit of the medieval sovereign, that he was well and graciously disposed toward her; in the second, using highly ornate and oddly interminable constructions, he told her the significance of his secret mission; and in the third he promised: "As, however, the great secrecy and indescribable importance of my duties, to my profoundest regret, makes it entirely impossible and unattainable to permit you to take part in the assembly which will help establish the freedom of my people and my own fame, I invite you come to me at six or seven in the evening on – (here an approaching date was named). Then I will tell you and Mother as much as I can tell without turning traitor, not to people, for I have no fear of them, but to the splendid, lofty and just cause..." and this lengthy invitation was signed – it slipped by accident from the over-strained quill – "King Bohusch. Signed and sealed in Prague." When he read it through again the hunchback had to smile, and he was almost about to destroy the pages. Then he thought: no, it's a good joke, anyway, that it is, sealed the letter and took it to the post office himself. As he heard it fall into the box, he heaved a sigh of relief. –

Frantischka did not reply; but in truth Bohusch had not expected her to. He was convinced that she would come, chastened, to find the new Bohusch whose friendship would surely seem a great and undeserved present to her. He would forgive her slowly and with hesitation, and then no doubt they would stop frequenting the Malvasinka on Sundays and go somewhere where they could show themselves, among the throngs in the Orchard[24] or the Star[25]. – All that Bohusch thought quite fleetingly in the few intervals when he was not preoccupied with the greatness which had now become his duty, his life. It was a grueling duty: all the many important things which he had thought fitfully in the impoverished years had to be thought all at once now, surveyed all at once and then voiced one after the other. There was such a throng of opinions, memories and plans within him that a whole flock of them was always just about to escape from his lips, wild and ruthless like people escaping a burning

[24] Stromovka: oldest, very popular park near the fairgrounds.

[25] Stern (Star) Summer Palace (Czech *Letohrádek Hvězda*): Palace in the shape of a six-pointed star with a park which once contained a game preserve. The grounds are not far from the site of the Battle of the White Mountain, a turning point in the history of the country. Here the Catholic League, led by the Imperial Commander Johann Count von Tilly, defeated the Estate troops of the Winter King Friedrich of Palatinate, thus clearing the way for 300 years of Habsburg rule in Bohemia.

theater. Then Bohusch put on a severe face and commanded with an air of superiority: "Quiet, one at a time. Everyone will have his turn." And just on these occasions the whole crowd would vanish, simply dissolve; Bohusch's mind went blank and he was incapable of thinking, much less saying a thing. Only after he had drunk a few glasses of hot *čaj* would the motley troop return, and the hunchback rejoiced and laughed until his eyes were filled with tears. All the while the ferment of his being grew and grew. He read many newspapers and old books, filled entire notebooks with his ludicrous letters, and in between these occupations, whether by day or at night, in a cafe or in a church, rarely at home, he snatched a few moments of wary sleep, soon starting up again as if in fright.

Thus approached the morning of the day on which Bohusch had promised the evening talk with his Mother and Frantischka, neither of whom would be able to share in his real triumph. He had passed the night in various taverns and beer-houses, and now he slunk past the houses haggard and bleary-eyed, peering foolishly, indifferently into the heavy rosy mist of the spring morning. He encountered few people. At the "Powder-Magazine"[26] two serving girls came toward him with big shopping

---

[26] Powder Magazine (Czech: *Prašná brána*): Gothic gate tower built in 1475 under Wladislaw II. Jagiello to replace the dilapidated Kuttenberg Gate from the 13th century, which straddled the road from the Old Town of Prague to the silver-mining town of Kuttenberg (Czech Kutná Hora).

baskets, laughing and chattering, and their eyes were so fresh and awake, their dresses and aprons still stiff from sheer newness. A little later he was overtaken by two infantrymen. They stepped out smartly, their steps clattered on the pavement in cheerful rhythm, and the buttons on their tunics stole the early sunbeams and tossed them impudently into Bohusch's sleepy eyes. Then some cheeky baker's boy whistled into the hunchback's face and laughed after him loudly, and a policeman sang something to himself, the feathers waving on his hat. Shutters rolled up with a rattle, and the plate-glass panes gave themselves up to the sun and burned in white flames. Through this fresh, cheerful explosion of life the cripple slunk pale and dissolute, with a creased shirt and filthy clothes, and he was like a loathsome poisonous toad discovered amidst sweetly fragrant beds. And he noticed nothing of this splendor but that it disturbed him, perhaps he was barely even aware that it was spring and morning. The riper this morning grew, the more one was struck by a certain excitement which all the people displayed. People who nodded at each other every day at this time without exchanging a word stopped, made concerned or astonished faces, shrugged their shoulders, and finally shook hands with a certain conventional gratitude, only to be stopped again ten steps on. People evidently felt the need to exchange some kind of information which was of concern and interest to all. At the corner of Ferdinandstrasse a policeman was reading a passage from the *Tschesky kurir*[27] to a circle of men and servant-girls, and a little further an elderly gentleman stepped outside a coffeehouse and said to his companion in German: "Extremely dangerous people, those. One ought to..." What one ought to do was no longer to be heard. The man walked along quite assuredly in very shiny shoes, and the younger man next to him nodded at every word, confirming it most assiduously; he seemed to be of exactly the same opinion. As Bohusch approached the "National" he saw Norinski through one window; in his heroic manner he seemed to be explaining something to the others, who could not be seen. For a while the hunchback hesitated. Then, instead of going inside, he walked down the quay to his apartment. He was tired.

In the meantime Norinski had come to a close. He drained his coffee – it might have been a cup of hemlock – with an extravagant gesture and said grandly: "None of you will say I'm not a good Czech. And I will take every opportunity to convince the wretched Germans of the contrary. Just let someone take that attitude with me. I'll put that gentleman's head on straight for him. But you mustn't play up these stories like that. That's nothing. That's childish nonsense, believe me." With that he rose, without paying for his breakfast, distributed his generous, three-act handshakes and betook himself across the street to his dressing room

---

[27] "Tschesky kurir": German spelling of *Český kurír*, a historic Czech newspaper.

with head held high. The remaining men drew together intimately, and Karás began to read aloud the various, brief newspaper articles relating to the incident. They all said more or less the same thing: a lady had put the police on the trail of a band of young people, students and journeymen, who held secret meetings in the cellar of a house on Hieronymousgasse, with treasonable speeches as the order of the day. Interestingly, girls were said to have taken part in these meetings as well. And German newspapers were gleeful at the destruction of this shameful criminal mob, regretting only that due to the defiant silence of the comrades who had been taken into custody, the brain behind this conspiracy had not yet fallen into the hands of the keepers of law and order, though thanks to the excellent training and acumen of the police this could not be long in coming. And finally, the German newspapers added, they hoped that a long-awaited example would be made of these young criminals and traitors and that ruthless action would be taken. All this they read in the "National". Schileder was honestly outraged: he said something about the courage of the young people and that rather than be content with producing words, fine words, they wanted to act as well. He did not put it well, and fell silent, cowed, when he met with none too lively agreement. For a moment they all nodded, his friends, and slipped some little word or other, like shamefaced alms, into the hand of righteousness. But in the end they all looked about

– they were so temptingly alone, and so they could afford to make a few confessions. Pátek condemned this cave romanticism out of hand; it no longer had any justification even in novels. And the poet Machal, who had only the vaguest notion of what had happened, yawned and remarked between two attempted yawns that to him the whole affair seemed brutal, terribly brutal. Karás, who felt more cosmopolitan every day, made a long speech during which his "Adam's apple" climbed up and down like a tree-frog plagued by doubts. The upshot of it was that to the outside, given the state of affairs, one must do everything to uphold the view that these young people were not merely martyrs for their idea, but the fallen heroes of a national cause, though he himself – here – could not but condemn such immature acts, he would say it straight out – immature acts – on the part of half-grown lads. One was too educated for that sort of thing, one knew that one could better uphold one's rights with great national commitments in life and in the political theater (a word which Karás constantly used in his feuilletons) than with such impertinences. No doubt he had more fluent phrases up his sleeve, but suddenly he stopped. He himself did not know why. The others looked up, and Rezek stood before them. The student, his dark eyes burning in his pale face, ignored the hands which were extended to him. Perhaps he had heard the critic's last words, but he made no reply, calmly took his accustomed seat and drank his *čaj*. At last Pátek began to

speak of a new book, and the artists lost themselves entirely in this discussion. A young colleague was hoping to publish several novellas
in the style of Maupassant. There were still
some difficulties regarding the financing and
other publishing matters, and they debated
whether to assist the author. The powerful
Karás was little inclined, and Pátek cried in
indignation: "But I beg you, that's a national
question!"

Rezek rose with an icy smile. "Are you Czechs?"
he asked.

They all fell silent and looked at each other
in confusion. Schileder got to his feet.

"Are you Czechs?" the student repeated.

Karás mollified: "Whatever are you thinking,
Rezek? Don't provoke."

"But you're ripe? Are you?" he went on. "Ripe
and ready."

"He's drunk," Machal whispered contemptuously.

Rezek clenched his fists. But he restrained
himself: "I know you're used to taking righteous anger for common drunkenness. I know.
But there is one thing I want to say to you, our
people is *not* ripe, and if you feel ready as you
are, you are its foes, you're traitors."

"I am an officer," said Pátek in a fearful
voice, stepping forward.

Rezek shook one fist in his face and walked
past him out of the room without saying a
word. –

Bohusch could hardly expect Frantischka
before six or seven o'clock, as he had told her in

his letter; by three o'clock, though, he began to wonder why his beloved hadn't come, by four he was about to go and fetch her, reluctantly abandoning the idea out of pride or for some other reason. With his hands behind his back he roamed around the little rooms whose profusion of ancestral furniture – they had taken far too much – from the porter's apartment posed considerable obstacles to his pacing. Now and then he stopped near the window at which a little old woman sat and sewed.

"Mama," he blurted out at last in torment, "you'll have to go and fetch her!"

The old woman nodded, removed her big round glasses and nodded. She did not give it a moment's thought: of course, she had to go fetch Frantischka. And she put on a hat in place of the bonnet and wrapped a good yellow shawl around her crooked shoulders. "You can say you just happened to be passing by, you... oh, God – well, you just happened to be passing by. Right? Why shouldn't you happen to pass by? I'm sure lots of people pass that way." Bohusch laughed abortively. "Well, tell me," he flared up in impatient rage, "is that possible?" Mrs. Bohusch nodded, thoroughly intimidated: "You know, first I'll go to the church next door. Then I can say I was in the church..." Still she hesitated. Bohusch's mind was elsewhere now. He barely noticed the old woman anymore, and was almost startled when his pacing took him up in front of her. The yellow shawl was unbearably dazzling in the afternoon sun. They looked at each other silently for a time, these two small, stunted people. Then the old woman toddled to the door and nodded and nodded. Suddenly Bohusch was at her side. *"Maminko"*[28], he said, and his voice was like that of a sick child. And the old, frightened woman understood. She grew, she became rich, she became a mother. This one quiet word made her so. Suddenly all the fearfulness in her was goodness, and the woman who had just now looked so vulnerable and helpless was powerful as she gently opened her arms, and for Bohusch it was like a homecoming. He nestled his great, heavy, wild head against her breast, he shut his hot eyes, he went under in this deep, unending love. He was silent. And then something within him burst out weeping. He heard just how it began. It must have been very deep inside him, it was so quiet. And it did not hurt. Then he opened his eyes in curiosity; he wanted to see where the weeping was. And behold: The weeping was not in him at all, it was his mother. At that Bohusch could not close his lids: tears waited behind them, many tears. – All at once it was so festive in the room. The things all around the two poor people took on a splendor which they had never possessed, not even in their princely days. Every pitcher, every little glass in the stiff étagère suddenly had its own light and boasted with it and wanted to play at being stars. One can well imagine that it grew very bright.

---

[28] Vocative of Czech *maminka* (affectionate form of *Mama*).

Then the clock struck gingerly, as if it regretted having to do so. But it struck five all the same, and the mother went.

"Where are you going?" quavered Bohusch.

"I must go fetch Frantischka." At that Bohusch remembered everything. He hesitated, then said almost sadly:

"That's right, you must go fetch Frantischka."

That was their parting.

Once Bohusch was alone, he started his nervous, restless pacing once more. Now and then, as if in passing, he put something straight, brushed the dust from the tablecloth and lost himself unexpectedly in putting his papers and books in order. He grew quite warm in the process. And when he found his hot face in a mirror somewhere, he was astonished. He wore his mother's dazzling yellow silk shawl draped about his shoulders. That was funny. He wanted to laugh, but it slipped his mind, and with involuntary movements of contentment he nestled his back still deeper into the soft folds. He felt weary, and in the parlor he dropped broad and heavy into the flowered cushions of the stiff chaise lounge which took up the middle of the room along with the oval table. He thought and thought. The poor festive chaise lounge groaned beneath him. He jumped to his feet, smoothed the crocheted coverlet with a certain tenderness, and took one of the chairs which stood to the side. His face, which could be boyish at times, aged minute by minute now with the intensity of his musings, virtually consumed by the wrinkles which crept across it and burrowed their way into it like caterpillars on a sick fruit. Did he really know everything he was going to say? A vague fear hung over him. He felt so deserted, dizzy, like someone forgotten atop a high tower. He groped for some hold. And after a while he began to imagine that by waiting in *this* place he was disrupting the order, the festive order of the room. His presumptuousness horrified him. He crept back further and further, finally crouching on a high-legged stool in the corner of the room, near the door. There peace descended upon him. He thought: So, now it's over; I've told everything already, and yet he knew that he had only wept, and that sort of weeping is quite different than speech. Nonetheless he insisted defiantly: I've told everything, mother knows everything – "and so do you" – he added out loud, seeking the eyes of the yellow cat which approached him slowly and slyly from the opposite corner. Not a claw grated against the brown, gleaming floorboards. The animal approached without a sound, it grew big, it grew bigger, and when Bohusch could no longer see past it into the silent, festive parlor, he fell asleep. And he must have dreamed. For he said in a voice which sounded far away: "That's it, Rezek, please – that's the secret: the painter must paint the people and tell it: you are beautiful." His head fell forward, and he lifted it with an effort. "The writer must write the people and tell it: you are beautiful." He sighed in his dreams: "Beauty is the thing."

Then a smile began in the corners of his mouth, a good, pious smile which grew across the sleeper's face and made it young again. He breathed: "I will never tell," and then his dream went so deep that not another word of it rose to his lips.

The door opened. But the hunchback did not open his eyes until Rezek grabbed him roughly by the throat and screamed very close: "Did you keep silent?" Bohusch felt these words hot on his cheek. His hands fended off spasmodically, but still there was no understanding in his eyes. They smiled still. They smiled at the terrible avenger until they died. And then the yellow shawl slid over the poor body and covered Bohusch and his secret. –

The Siblings

Around noon the new tenants moved into the old house across from the Church of the Order of Malta – up three flights of stairs – and by evening all anyone knew was that they had brought unusually large furniture which had almost gotten stuck in the narrow windings of the spiral stairs. And the old watery-eyed peddler woman who sat nearby under the dark stone arcade could hardly get over the thought of the enormous oak wardrobes; she swore to the neighbors that these had been "aristocratic" wardrobes. This declaration sparked an unusual excitement in the house in question, keeping the many tenants on tenterhooks: every few moments a slovenly woman came out of one of the white-painted doors, on each of which a few grimy calling-cards clustered around a metal or glass nameplate, and cocked an ear up the stairs, shrinking back in shame if she happened to encounter another eavesdropper there, who in turn would be about to retreat in alarm until they recognized each other as kindred souls and goaded on their own hungering curiosity with dark conjectures.

But suddenly the female population was drawn to the courtyard windows and away from the narrow stairwell which grew up through the walls like a spine. Deep down below in the

cylindrical courtyard, as if at the bottom of a well, a hurdy-gurdy began to sob out the melody from the *Beggar Student,* and already a few children – no one knew where they came from – had gathered around the old drunkard to perform a strange and wild dance. After some agonized groaning, the notes came like belches from the organ's dry throats, seemed to shoot up and tug like invisible lassoes at all the necks which sprouted to unbelievable lengths from the dormers and kitchen windows, relieving the bareness of the walls like some bizarre architectural ornamentation. In the twilight the women who greeted each other from all sides resembled one another like peas in a pod; as if in wary mimicry their faces all seemed to have taken on the indescribably hideous color of the walls, and even their movements and their voices were of such a startling uniformity that they seemed appendages of the house rather than free-moving individuals. One might have supposed that the object of all the heads' attention was the pathetic hurdy-gurdy, for some even nodded along with the music; in reality, though, all eyes took root on the fourth-floor kitchen window, and many a credulous ear seemed to hear the scrape of its latch. The hurdy-gurdy exhausted itself with a gallop to which a little black dog howled the accompaniment, the organ-grinder bellowed his thanks and dragged himself away. The bright flock of children trailed after him like a chain, and suddenly all sensed the silence and the darkness of the musty courtyard. But just in this strangely attentive moment the longed-for window opened almost noiselessly, and the old maidservant Rosalka leaned way out. Almost all the heads vanished, only one pert, impatient voice called: "Well, finished moving in?" The maidservant Rosalka merely nodded, and just as the hurdy-gurdy quietly began to play something very wistful in a neighboring house, the old woman settled in the black window like a big sad bird and dropped the life story of her master and mistress down into the listening courtyard, negligently, like potato peels. And even if no one could be seen at the windows now, not one of her broad words was lost to the walls, from which an encouraging question would rise now and then. An hour later, when the Order of Malta rang Ave, even the old peddler in the stone arcade knew the entire fate of the forester's widow Josephine Wanka and her two children, and she passed it on to her last, daily customers, the chancery clerk Jerabek and the lackey Dvorak, along with the "aristocratic" wardrobes.

But perhaps the ladies' thirst would have been stilled even without the old woman's general confession. For the three people who had left tiny Krummau for the capital wore their memories and experiences over their clothes, as it were; one needed only brush them to take a piece away. In part, no doubt, this was due to the ways of the small town, where all deck themselves out with their happiness and wear their sorrow as visibly as possible; if anyone is imprudent enough to hold himself aloof, both joy and sorrow alike will be dragged from their secret hiding place by the neighbor's pitiless hands, and then he may see whether he recognizes his quiet joy or silent sorrow in the rumor distorted by hatred and derision. But the Wanka family's frankness was more likely due to the fact that – though a year had passed since then – the most recent and momentous event of their lives still hung over them. Especially in the women's faces one still saw the signs of fate, the marks of its brutal clutch, and fear always lurked somewhere in the background of their voices, only to spread suddenly, without reason, over all their words. But the son Zdenko, about twenty years old, had something serious and reserved in his stern face which quickly robbed him of all sympathy. The fact that – as everyone heard in the first few days – he was a medical student brought him, rather than good will, a certain grudging respect which he seemed neither to notice nor to rebuff. But even if the women, by their very nature, betrayed themselves constantly, they still maintained a certain coolness toward their obliging neighbors; weeks had passed since that first day, and not a single neighbor had gained entry to the rooms of the widowed Mistress Forester. Being so unattainable, this had gradually become a goal to which all aspired in hot competition; disdaining no ruse, they came late in the evening to ask the Wankas for a sugar-mortar or a corkscrew, which they misplaced with puzzling frequency, or as last resort the key to the attic, things which they usually took away together with the irritation at not having seen past the threshold of the living room.

This intractable obstinacy was all out of proportion to the old maidservant's original confessions, and understandably enough her obligingness was expected to provide all the rest. But she too seemed to grow more taciturn and mistrustful and, when pressed, would always start telling the story everyone knew by now: about the March morning on which the woodcutters had carried the district forester Joachim Wanka home from the forest, shot by poachers. And that his face was filled with congealed anger and lay dark as if in the shadow of his bushy eyebrows, and how his fists would not unclench, not even in all the tears, so that one day at the Last Judgement the forester would have much ado to act as if he had been lying there with piously folded hands the whole time. Then the old woman crossed herself with a roughness born of habit and insisted for good measure that long before it happened she had foreseen the whole tragedy from dreams and signs, and because Master Julius Caesar[29] had begun to haunt Krummau Castle again and the castellan had seen Emperor Rudolf[30] sitting in an armchair across from him, resting his

[29] Julius Caesar: According to an old legend, Emperor Rudolf II's mad son, called Julius Caesar, pursued a burgher's daughter until she threw herself from a window of the tower of Krummau castle.

[30] Emperor Rudolf: The son of Emperor Maximilian II, Rudolf II (1552-1612) ruled as the King of Bohemia from 1575, residing in the Prague Castle. In the Rudolfine Period art and scholarship flourished in Prague.

68

head on his hand and gazing across the nocturnal Vltava valley at the stars.

Old Rosalka had no use for those who did not believe in such things; she held that to be a lack of education and experience and one of the many evil consequences which was making ever greater strides "in the big city". In the evening, when Mrs. Wanka had what seemed very serious and circumspect talks with her son, she could not help motioning the daughter Luisa, who sat there perfectly superfluous with big forlorn eyes, into the kitchen and warning her of the sinful mouths of the heretics who had no awe of anything anymore – neither graveyard nor midnight, not even both of them at once. And soon the old woman had conjured up the atmosphere in which she was at home: the things all around, from the stiff kitchen cabinet to the unwieldy washing trough, which just now had stood there so prosaically, suddenly began to listen, and they seemed to draw closer and closer to the two women so as not to miss a single word of Rosalka's, noises like footsteps woke, and an old tin pan laughed for no reason: "plink!" Then the maidservant paused, and with pounding hearts the two harked to the silvery sound, and it seemed to them than an invisible clock had struck some significant hour. And sometimes, as if in collusion with Rosalka, the old kitchen lamp would go out just as they were listening, and the rich twilight grew heavy and close with a thousand giddy possibilities. Luisa, who always sat silently in the corner, grew smaller and smaller in the face of these powers; she seemed to dissolve, leaving nothing behind but two large anxious eyes which followed the apparitions with a certain trustfulness. Then she seemed to be in the great ballroom of Krummau Castle whose walls are painted with life-size figures all the way up to the vaulted, echoing ceiling. Many hundreds of years ago, it is said, a French painter contrived these carnival groups so skillfully, in such rich and startling variety that even in broad daylight one constantly sees new, fantastically-costumed guests appear behind each figure. In Krummau all are convinced that this is due not to the artist's skill but to the strange fact that at a certain hour the knights and ladies come to life and repeat the drama of that one long-ago night. Emerging from the walls, their shimmering throng fills the hall. Until the enormous grenadiers at the doors of the hall slam their halberds against the floor: then they fall into rows. A clap of thunder rolls over them. Prince Julius Caesar, the second Rudolf's secret son, has drawn up at the jutting ramp with his six wild black horses, and barely a moment later he stands black and slender amidst the deeply, deeply bowing guests like a cypress in a field of waving grain. Then the music shuffles the crowd, an alien music which seems to arise from the brushing-together of the costly dresses and, swelling, lifts from the masses broad and roaring like the melody of a sea. And here and there the prince motions apart the gleaming waves, vanishes in them, rises from them proudly in the far corner, lets his radiant smile play over them like a flash of sunlight and tosses a bright, wanton word into the billows like a precious ring which all snatch at. And in the wilder, wallowing to-and-fro the secret desire grows... The prince sees a pale, blue lady at a silver knight's side, and feels at once: the love of her, the hatred of her companion. And both are red and quick in him. And he has made the silver knight a king, it seems; for purple flows down his shining armor, growing broader and more bloody until he collapses silently under the weight of his princely cloak: "Thus fares many a king," the prince laughs into his dying eyes. At that the festive figures freeze in horror and fade slowly and fearfully back into the dimming walls, and the abandoned hall rises from the last shining waves like a land of bleached cliffs. Only Julius Caesar is left behind, and the greedy glow of his hot eyes scorches the pale lady's senses. But when he makes to seize her she tears herself from his compelling gaze and flees into the black, echoing hall; her light blue silk gown is left behind, torn, like a piece of moonlight in the prince's wild hands, and he wraps it around his neck and throttles himself with it. He gropes after her into the night, and suddenly he shouts with joy. He hears that she has discovered the little hidden door, and he knows: now she is his; for there is only one way she can go from there: the narrow tower stairs which lead to the fragrant little round chamber – high in the Vltava tower. And in wanton haste he is at her heels, always at her heels, and though he does not hear her fleeing steps, he sees her before him like a radiance at every turn of the stairs. Then he seizes her again, and now he holds the filmy fear-warm slip in his hands, only the slip, and it is cool to his lips and cheeks. His head spins, and as he kisses his booty he falters and leans against the wall. Then with three or four tiger leaps he looms in the door of the tower room and – freezes: high before the night rears the white pure body, naked, as if blossomed from the window-frame. And neither of them moves. But then, before he can think, two bright childishly frail arms rise into the stars as if to become wings, something flickers out before him, and there is nothing in the high window arch but the hollow howling night and a cry...

"And you're eighteen, are you really?" said Zdenko, bending over his terrified, weeping little sister, so small and shy that she almost vanished in the corner of the kitchen. "So your old ghosts have followed you here to Prague? Or did Rosalka bring them along in her pots and pans?" The old maidservant turned away, grumbling. "Yes," Luisa hesitated, "yes," and took a halting breath, "when we first came here I thought I was rid of them. When I saw the bright houses and the wide streets I felt so free and happy, but here in the Lesser Quarter it's almost worse than home. Isn't it?" And the girl looked around slowly. But Zdenko pulled her after him into the living room. "Of course, just as I told you," he called to his mother, "while we're talking in here she's out there with the old witch again, all worked up from this eternal nonsense." Mrs. Josephine softly shook her head with its broad streaks of grey and said: "When will you ever come to reason, my child?" She sewed away calmly at pieces of white linen, and still more work waited in the basket beside her. But after a while the widow laid her needle-pricked hands in her lap and looked her daughter in the face. Blinded by the bright lamp, Luisa had shut her eyes, and in her pale delicate little face lingered a fear so vivid that her mother took alarm. Suddenly she realized how slight and frail the girl was, and she wondered whether she would have the strength to walk upright in life without help and support one day. The mother's kindly pale-blue eyes dulled with tears, though it could have been exhaustion; for plain-work is toilsome, and Mrs. Wanka's eyelids were always reddened from it. After a while Luisa, no doubt sensing her gaze, began to help her mother. The two women bent over the linen, and the hanging lamp shone harshly on the grey and the blonde heads. Now Zdenko said: "I don't know, it always seems to me that Luisa has stayed so small out of sheer awe. Really. It could be. If someone's always surrounded by such tremendous things from childhood on – just think of the castle on the steep cliffs, these lofty courtyards, the great cannons on the bulwarks, and finally the halls full of chairs and pictures and vases which seem made for giants – he either grows to match these things..."

(Mrs. Wanka smiled her son in the face and then went on sewing zealously) "or – he loses all the courage to match them. Thinking: I will never be that big. And the days pass in sheer gazing and wonderment, and you forget yourself and that these things are really only an example. Don't you think so, Luisa?"

"Maybe," his sister nodded without pausing in her work.

"I also felt how oppressive that can be – as a boy." Zdenko gazed past the women into the unknown. "But one day comes the jolt, when you stand on tip-toes in front of all that instead of kneeling to it, and once you've managed that it's not long before you're gazing beyond it. And believe me, that makes all the difference. Always look beyond everything. The one who stands the highest is always the master. I've always had quite a clear notion of what makes our time so confused and so uncertain; but now that I live here in the city and see so many people – I know: it's that no one stands above it all. You'll tell me that's wrong: over the city is the mayor and over him the governor, and has a long way to look up to the king and the king to the emperor and he to the pope. But the pope, even with his thrice-lofty crown, still doesn't reach up to the Good Lord, you'll say. I think that's because people usually see the matter the wrong way around. It seems to me that the Good Lord is way down at the bottom, and a little bit above him is the pope and so on. But at the top is the people. And the people is many, not one; they push and shove one another, and one blocks the other's sun. That's what I always think – from time to time they must lift someone up, not too high (otherwise he could fall down where the king is or the emperor), but so that he feels their strong and faithful shoulders beneath him and can gaze over their heads for a while in calm deliberation. But when he stands in their midst again it will be as if he has returned from the homeland and can tell his brothers where the sun rises and how long it may take until then – and many other things. But this way..." Zdenko covered his eyes with one hand. Then he rose energetically: "Mmh, enough of the drudgery, go to sleep; it's late. And the lamp is about to go out." His voice was rough. Only now did he realize that Luisa was no longer bent over her linen; her eyes blazed at him, big and radiant as never before. And strange, he saw himself in these eyes and drew himself up, proud and strong, as if in front of a mirror.

But his mother sewed all the while in nimble, never-resting toil, and suddenly Zdenko felt the urge to go up to her and kiss her hands.

It was not mistrust which had made the maidservant Rosalka turn curt and closemouthed toward her neighbors. This often happens to old people when they are driven from the accustomed petty domesticity of their provincial town and are forced to find their way in a new place; unable to adapt themselves to the larger scale, they seem to have been transported from a small chamber into an echoing hall in which their most secret words are loudly repeated as if by invisible choirs. At first they enjoy the novelty of it, but soon it becomes an effort which, without sufficient reward, only disheartens, and one morning they leave their hands on their laps and their words on their tongues. Moreover, country people are a good deal more modest. There one really respectable misfortune suffices to draw the reverent pity of one's acquaintances for all time like a lifelong rent, until one's last blessed day. But "in the big city" – grumbled the old woman – you had to lose a father at least once a week and fall down the stairs or out of the window every three weeks just to keep halfway in form. With misty eyes she thought of her "position" in Krummau and could not forgive her mistress for moving to Prague so that Zdenko could attend the university. She did not take it amiss that the Mistress Forester had to go to "households" herself a few times a week, supplementing her small pension and the allowance from the princely Schwarzenbergs to earn what was necessary for the new household and her son's education. She also knew that Mrs. Wanka would spare no sacrifice for Zdenko and harbored the dark desire to see him become a "learned doctor", which struck Rosalka as the improper ambition of an unbridled vainglory at the sight of which one ought to cross oneself three times over.

The widow's aspirations were regarded differently in the household of Frau Oberst a. D. Meering von Meerhelm, where the forester's wife mended the fine linens every Monday, on washing day. Frau Charlotte Meering praised the mother's zeal and only faulted the fact that Zdenko had entered the Bohemian and not the German university. This obvious mistake was to blame for the fact that he could never be invited to visit. In vain did the widow protest that all this had been in accordance with the wishes of her poor departed husband, a good Czech; the Oberstin only smiled genteelly, unable, as she put it to her husband, to "understand these people's narrow-mindedness". To make up for it Luisa was sometimes allowed to come for her mother and, if she promised to speak only German, spend ten minutes "playing" with the Meering children, a fifteen-year-old rascal and his sister Lizzie, about three years younger. Admittedly the results were always rather different; the two siblings would pounce on the shy and timorous girl and begin to push and shove her like some inanimate object. Usually Frau von Meering would appear in the door of the nursery just as Luisa, tied to a closet, represented a white victim and her offspring leaped about Indian-style with wild whoops of triumph. Not surprisingly, Luisa did not look forward to these visits in the least and was thankful when her mother let her wait in the vestibule or on the street. Sometimes the Herr Obrist would pass her on his way home and stop in front of the girl for a moment, postponing the horrors of washing day. The short, stout gentleman, who wore a great sense of honor on the inside and a great medal on the outside of his chest, would puff up his mousta-che contentedly and always began the brief conversation like this:

"Waiting for your beau, young lady?"

At that Luisa would always turn as red as the poor light of the alley necessitated. This delighted the old gentleman, who appreciated the exquisiteness of his joke more keenly every time; he was always glad to repeat it to his Lotti at dinner, after the children had gone to bed, of course. Aside from that he had little to tell. There was something pensive in his na-ture, as this example will show. He had spent more than five years wondering about the meaning of the sign he was occasionally given from above. Of course, he did not understand it until much later, when the ceaseless signing in higher places had already stirred up a kind of storm which finally wafted the Herr Obrist gently from the dangerous pinnacle of regi-mental command and into the tranquil valley of retirement where he now rambled, pensive as before. He was a man who judged the depths of existence by the awful abysses of almanac tales, and often wondered at the height he had reached, in defiance of all dangers, on the earth-ly ladder of rank. Righteous by nature, not only did he admire himself unreservedly, he treated all according to their worth and merit. Having learned that the deceased Wanka had been a princely forester and that Mrs. Josephine had occasionally been obliged to take the place of the lady-in-waiting in Frauenberg Castle, he welcomed the widow in his home and felt that this family breathed out indirect princely grace.

When Mrs. Wanka finally stepped out the door of the Meerings' house, weary-eyed, on these Monday evenings, she would give her daughter a kiss and the two women would walk through the lively streets of the New Town toward the stone bridge, usually without speaking a word. Only once they had turned off the loud Brückengasse into the narrow, barely-lit side streets were their voices released, and they would begin to speak of Zdenko softly and slowly, like two music-boxes dreaming timid songs in the middle of the night. Their conversations were filled with a loyal, touching tenderness all the more ardent because it never descended into words, but filled the women completely, making their movements beautiful and their smiles more luminous. Since that evening when Luisa's eyes had caught fire so strangely at her brother's hot words, he had become a different person for her, powerful, and though Mrs. Wanka's love for her son flowed from different springs, mother and daughter understood each other in this low, listening speech, telling each other in many words more or less this: he has become a different person.

They were right about that. A joyful excitement had come over the young man. His friendship with the forest and the vigorous calm of his parental home had bestowed gifts upon him, over and over again, and what was asked of him was so absurdly little. When he thought of the years before his father's death he was now inclined to believe that he had really known one single day which appeared again and again after every night, replete and satisfied – until the first great woe: his dear father's violent death. Past that lay something lifeless and empty which was like a respite or a forgetting. But then in the midst of it – so he felt – a door, a gate had opened somewhere, and now they stormed in, all the young bright days, holding their hands out to him in impatient appeal. How grateful he was for their desire! He stood there like a homecomer, handing out gifts on all sides, and the things are from so far away, and each of the recipients knows just what to do with them. Wanka felt that the whole world was living out of his pockets, and living well at that. He was always surrounded by a circle of young people to whom he tossed out serious and mischievous ideas pell-mell, and all found enough there to fill their days and nights. He failed to notice the aimlessness of these young minds; he himself had no aim, for he had a thousand of them, taking up this one today and that one tomorrow. This way of life threw him together with a great many people; he devoted himself to all of them with equal devotion, and whenever he felt truly inspired by a new thought of his, he felt he had the mistrustful bystanders to thank for it. Little by little he grew quieter, began to listen attentively to dissenting opinions as well, and found that he was not really capable of replying to them. Slowly he began to realize that all his enthusiasms were fragments of a great

monologue, and this insight sobered him greatly and made him lonely.

Now he spent whole nights sitting silently in the Cafe National at the table which was frequented by men older and graver than he, whom he believed to be the vanguard of the people. They were writers and painters, actors and students. They all had a certain affectation which once had violently repelled him, but now he tried to accustom himself to it. After the theater they gathered, tired and surly, and gave each other pitying smiles in greeting. Their clothes were either exaggeratedly elegant or grossly unkempt, and at first glance it was hard to tell what united them. A few glasses of *čaj* or Budweiser beer made it apparent that the similarity lay in the big words which escaped from their lips the more profusely and impetuously the later it grew. One difference remained, however: the ones in the fashionable clothes merely laid their words on the table in front of them, as it were, with the warning: do not touch. The others just threw them into the air, little caring whom they might hit. Wanka heard the affairs of the "nation" debated, he learned for the first time of its distress and need, of its silent fervent yearning. Suddenly he was overcome with shame like a laughing man who learns that there has been a death in the house, and he wondered how he could have failed to notice this oppression all these years. He thirsted to learn ever so much about it, but when he turned back to the men he found that they had long since moved on to other things, speaking of art and the like in exactly the same tone of voice. And all at once he saw that their enthusiasm was nothing but vehemence, and that they had nothing in common but their conceit. At that he withdrew from them. He stayed at home again in the evening, devoted himself more zealously to his studies at the university, and imagined for a while that all was as it had been. Until on one such evening, by sheer chance, he put words to his innermost thoughts, as he had the time he found Luisa in the kitchen with her ghosts. Since then he knew he met the eyes of the people on the street in a different way, searching their faces for traces of the suffering which was said to afflict his people. Here and there he thought he really did see a dejected, oppressed figure, but when he looked closer he saw that only the burden of poverty or misery rested on the strange shoulders, not the yoke of oppression. And yet it refused to leave him in peace. He still felt forces within him, and asked himself every day whether his people might need them. He grew increasingly perplexed and discontent, and endured neither the lecture hall nor the sitting room where Luisa sat waiting for him with big questioning eyes. So he went on long walks.

Once, in the spring, he walked through the Podskal[31], lost in thought, and when he looked up a grey monolithic building loomed up before him in the midst of a partly torn-up lot, its

---

[31] Podskal, Czech *Podskalí* ("under the cliffs"): A suburb of Prague.

windows staring at him emptily, as if burned out. Wanka took it for a former barracks now facing demolition, and as the area did not seem to be closed off, he entered through one of the yawning gates. The yards were filled with doors and door-frames, boards and all kinds of old scrap, and these things looked unbelievably sad in the dull, slowly fading light of the late afternoon. The student turned away and, guided by some vague feeling, climbed the worn-down wooden stairs and walked down long white corridors and through many white-washed rooms with low ceilings and partly torn-up floors. And then he climbed another flight of stairs and stood in another corridor; at the end of it the wall was torn away and the wind came in wide from the grey day. It tore straws from the rafters of the ceiling and drove them at the stranger like arrows. Wanka went straight through one of the next doors and found himself in a cramped cell barely three strides across and not much longer, evenly filled with the meager light which flowed in through a barred opening close to the ceiling. The white-grey walls were covered with cracks like a strange crazed pattern, and it was a moment before the student realized that this pattern resolved itself into words and images; he read prayers and curses, names and places, all scratched onto wild, grinning faces, strangely intertwined with the lines of their noses and eyes, more like eloquent folds and wrinkles than like writing. And one face grew out behind the other, pale and trembling; coming to life, the wall surged toward him like a mob, led by a threatening, angry man with hollow eyes. And across his brow stood: "Jesus Mary".

Then Wanka heard someone say his name. In indescribable horror he turned as if to flee, and ran up hard against Rezek[32], the pale student, who said with a peculiar, knowing smile: "These were artists too. Don't you think?"

Wanka, recognizing the student, stared at him uncomprehending.

"Well, I mean, each in his own way," the other smiled. Then he added seriously: "Believe me, these pictures are closer to my heart than what our painters paint and our writers dream up. Do you know what these are? Folk songs. Not from a thousand years ago, nor incomprehensible ten thousand years later. Poems in an eternal tongue. These walls ought to be lifted out like the walls of hieroglyphs in the pyramids. They ought to be hung in the churches; for they are holy. Look here," and he touched his hard, slender finger to a drawing which showed a small house with clumsy strokes; "yearning made that, and faith wrote a prayer beneath it, and despair a curse, and derision, with torn bloody nails, drew a hideous face around it, making the dear little house look like a greedy, wide-open mouth. – Have you ever seen a more horrifying picture?"

"Come," said Wanka, seized by sudden fear.

Rezek followed. "I come here often," he said. "The razing goes so slowly. I read from these

---

[32] Rezek: one of the central characters in "King Bohusch".

walls as from the Book of Revelation. I've found answers to many questions there."

They fell silent. "Of course," Rezek added as they walked out the gate, "in the end the answer itself is another question. But only one, always the same, and that's not as terrible as all the many."

"What is this building, anyway?" Wanka asked now, turning back to the abandoned structure which stood against the evening black and huge with its many empty windows.

Rezek looked up: "The old St. Wenceslas Penitentiary." He stopped to light a cigarette. Then they walked silently toward the city.

Now the two young people, who once had passed each other by, began to meet almost every day. But Wanka was drawn to his somber fellow-student less of his own volition than by a power over his will; and what held him then was that Rezek divined all the questions which had tormented him lately, answering the unspoken ones instinctively. To be sure, Zdenko failed to see how far these answers went beyond his questions, and so it soon happened that his strength and the naive cleverness of his unspoiled youth blindly served the energetic agitator, for whom they must have been most opportune. The increased vigilance of the police, the "King Bohusch" affair and other semi-political incidents had made the young people cautious and fearful, and for some of his ends Rezek had to use the paid rabble who turned informer at the very next opportunity. But the dark man's dream was this: to find uncorrupted young people of good family who, convinced of the righteousness of their undertaking, would fight for national liberation with all the blind brute force of their convictions, pursuing with youthful dauntlessness a goal in which he himself could not always believe.

On their walks together, which Luisa joined, listening, they had discovered a small, unfrequented taproom high up in the Hradschin. From their round window bay they often watched the heavy, hazy spring evenings destroy the city, its fire consuming the towers and cupolas, flaring here and there like madness from two brooding window eyes. And the whole burden of these foreboding dusks weighed upon the three young people; then the energetic Rezek, who had a great fear of these quiet expansive hours, would turn to the pensive girl and say in a hard voice: "Loisinka, play something for us." And the long notes of a harmonium would sough like wing-beats from the niche where Luisa sat, and the simple folksongs made the people still quieter and lonelier. It grew darker and darker around them, and they felt like people parting, waving to each other though none now can make the other out... Until the song broke off in the middle of a note and the tremulous subsiding of the harmonium merged with Luisa's timid tears. Then Rezek commanded: "Play something cheerful..."

But Luisa knew only a few folksongs, and her brother said: "Our people has no light-hearted songs. Its favorite songs seem about to weep."

Rezek began to stride fiercely up and down the little room; at last he stopped in the window bay and said:

"Our people is like a child. Sometimes I see that: our hatred toward the Germans really is nothing political at all, it's something – how should I put it? – something human. Our grievance is not that we must share our homeland with the Germans, what makes us sad is that we must grow up amidst such a full-fledged people. It's the story of the child growing up among old people. It learns to smile before it's ever able to laugh."

But when the waitress had lit the lamp Rezek sat down in the big old armchair and began to speak as if to himself, pressing his nervous yellow hands to his eyes: "Back then, when they said to the people: you are young, the educated classes were ashamed of it. And they got old in a hurry, instead of getting older. Instead of delighting in each day, they had to have a yesterday and a day before. The Königinhof Manuscript[33], of course! Not content with that, they sought their culture abroad, right where it's most finished – in France. And so it happened: centuries lie between the educated Czechs

---

[33] Königinhof Manuscript: Literary documents forged at the beginning of the 19th century, consisting of epic and lyric poems supposedly from the 13th century. The forger, Václav Hanka, was inspired by nationalist motives. These supposed finds were of great importance for the Czech Romantics, inspiring the entire nation, though doubts as to their authenticity emerged from the outset. Hanka's forgery, which was followed by the Grünberg Manuscript, also forged, was exposed at the end of the 19th century by T. G. Masaryk, who was later to become the first president of the republic.

and the people. They no longer understand each other. As far as culture is concerned, we have nothing but dotards and children. Our beginning and our end come at the same time. We cannot last. *That* is our tragedy, not the Germans."

Luisa saw the horror which etched her brother's face at this confession. He seemed to restrain himself with an effort, all his sinews were taut as if to leap.

Rezek did not notice; he roused himself as if from a nightmare, and the stern tone of his voice seemed to recant all that had gone before. That evening he proposed the most daring plans, pursuing all chances and channels so ruthlessly with his unique acumen, seemed so clear in his mind about the aims of his tireless agitation, that Zdenko completely succumbed to his influence once again.

Nevertheless, this evening marked the beginning of a harsh inner struggle for Wanka. He had felt both strong and proud in his mission as long as he believed he was fighting for a young and healthy people; now he learned that this people suffered from inner discord and despaired in itself. And he lost all his joy and all his courage. He fared like the daring lieutenant who flings himself into the thick of overwhelming enemy forces at the head of his company. Then he learns that the defeat of his side is already sealed; and what was just a joyous act of heroism now seems a useless, desperate sacrifice. All at once the poor young man feels so much within him that is new, unused, lonely, that does not want to end and yearns to blossom again in another quiet spring. – The lofty, ringing words of national enthusiasm had faded in his ears, and more than once Wanka dashed off from the hot secret meetings and into the night alleys, where he strayed aimlessly toward an uncertain morning. But Rezek's personality held such sway over him that in the midst of his broodings he would expect Rezek to show him a way out, and did not dare to admit his growing doubts to that grim fellow. He spoke of them to no one. He saw the troubled inquiry in his simple mother's eyes, and thought he could drown it out with his hearty, hasty tenderness. He drew closer to his pale little sister, attempting to find himself, as it were, in these fleeting moments of pure love.

Now Luisa, full of foreboding, began to sense the conflict in Zdenko's soul. She knew nothing of his budding disloyalty to his work, nor that the duty he had shouldered had become duress. But she saw that he was wrenching at some kind of chains, and to her it seemed this was Rezek's implacable power which he fled again and again only to return weak and despondent. For some time now the figure of the pale man had held sway over her as well. She found his image in all her thoughts and was no longer surprised. He seemed to belong there like Christ on the Cross in the convent cell. And she could not stop him from growing into her dreams as well, becoming one with the dark prince in the old dream of the masquerade; for her he was no longer called Rezek, but

Julius Caesar. And now a strange thing happened to the girl. Certain scenes from far-off years, half-forgotten dreams and figures and strange purple words which she had heard from her brother, and other things which she could not explain at all, crowded around her like a new fantastic time in which all laws would be different, and all duties. No longer able to distinguish between deed and dream, she saw all the events of daily life in the colors of that Krummau masque of blood, her deepest and most shattering memory. Now she lived in the midst of the silent, solemn figures and felt more and more plainly that she too must have a role in this secret round. And for days she sat at the window with work forgotten on her lap, gazing at the high bare walls of the Church of the Order of Malta with lost eyes, and wondered: Which, though, which?

The languid summer days slowly drew toward the Feast of Assumption[34]. A leaden sadness came over the Wankas. Homesickness, which the four had almost forgotten, visited them again in another, unexpected form. They no longer yearned for the past; instead, in their hot rooms behind curtained windows, they dreamed of the light, airy village summer, so neighborly with the cool forests. Of the bright paths over the fields, crossed by the touchingly thin shadows of the young fruit trees, so that one

---

[34] Feast of Assumption: The Feast of the Assumption of the Virgin is celebrated on August 15.

walks over them as if on a ladder, from bar to bar. Of the ripe, heavy fields which begin such a broad and splendid surging toward dusk, and of the copses whose darkening silence hides taciturn ponds, no one knows how deep. And each of the four thought of some particular insignificant hour whose small happiness they had simply taken with them once without valuing it. And this longing was all the more painful as it was not for something unrecoverable, as each felt the serene native summer waiting for them and growing sad when no one came. To be closer to it, at least, they went on little excursions along the Vltava. The forester's widow was most receptive to the good-natured pastoral lie of the little woods outside Kuchelbad[35] and was filled with the imperceptible good cheer peculiar to hard-working old people. She was quiet and lost in thought and barely smiled, but the creases around her lips were gone, and that gave her face something young and sunny which perhaps she had not even had as a bride. And so she hardly noticed how rarely Zdenko raised his eyes from the rooty path to the bright landscape, how quickly the summer flowers wilted in Luisa's hot hands. Old Rosalka stayed at home altogether and sulked, saying: no, if the summer won't come to me, I won't go running after it. She sat at the

[35] Kuchelbad (Czech *Chuchle*): Suburb of Prague, popular weekend destination for Prague inhabitants, with a steamer dock. Chuchle, once the summer seat of the Prague bishops, is now famous for its racetrack.

kitchen window with an old prayer-book and fell asleep at her piety.

Only one person seemed unencumbered by the dusty August days: Rezek. His energy remained indefatigable; indeed, lately he even showed a streak of boisterous joviality which puzzled Wanka. Unaware that Rezek always became so unruly when danger loomed over him and his secret endeavors, he took the change as a sign that things were going well.

The three of them went walking once more, resuming their old custom; Rezek suggested stopping in the "Vikárka" (an ancient little tavern across from St. Vitus Cathedral), and Zdenko's last misgivings vanished. They sat at a dark table in the hindmost room and toasted each other with genuine Mělník[36]. The student did not stint with the wine, and his mirth waxed so loud that the few other guests, episcopal lackeys, were compelled to partake of it. Rezek told the legend of the Bread Countess[37] who was said to haunt the old Czernin Palace, insinuating his spiteful mockery at the tensest moments and altering the effect of his words in a strange and startling fashion. Here and there other tales came to life (they lurk in all the corners of these murky rooms), and it so happened that Zdenko told the Krummau legends, including the one about Julius Caesar.

[36] Mělník: The picturesque town of Mělník, a renowned Bohemian wine-growing town, lies at the confluence of the Vltava and the Elbe.

[37] Bread Countess: In an old legend, a vain countess insisted on standing out at a ball by arriving in shoes made of bread crusts — only to be punished by the Devil for her frivolity.

"More your metier, really," he said to Luisa first.

But she only shook her head mutely, raised the wineglass and held it to her lips for a long time. She began to sip with her mouth almost closed, and her wide eyes gazed into the drink which cast its purple reflection on her thin face.

Suddenly Rezek said: "How you tell it. Strange. Isn't there a similarity between our time and the eve of the Thirty Year's War?"

Something trembled beneath his words. Zdenko and several others laughed. But Luisa lifted the tumbler slowly from her cool red mouth and looked up at the student with frightened eyes.

Later, near the old stairs to the castle on the way home, Rezek stopped at a door with a black matrimonial coat of arms resplendent over its arch, and asked: "Were you ever inside?"

The siblings replied in the negative.

"Then you don't even know the Daliborka[38]? For shame."

And already Rezek had stepped through the narrow doorway, and Luisa, who was standing next to him, saw a tidy courtyard in which the broad warm shadows of the afternoon lay, guarded by the bright walls. A little woman came out of the house door with a greeting, shooed away a flock of chickens, and motioned the strangers to follow her. Zdenko went first, then came

---

[38] Daliborka: One of the turrets of the Prague Castle's northern fortifications, built to contain keeps and deep dungeons. One of the most famous prisoners was the Knight Dalibor from Kozojedy. Bedřich Smetana's romantic opera "Dalibor" popularized this historic figure outside the country as well.

Rezek, followed by Luisa, for the path was so narrow that they had to go single file. Luisa hung back a little and looked around with shining eyes: there was an absurdly small vegetable garden whose cabbage heads and asparagus spears a six-year-old child could have counted; but in the middle reared a sturdy apple tree which seemed to show its small red fruits to the distant shimmering city. A few overgrown steps led down a damp, dim stretch of the slope, full of wild rosebushes whose branches refused to let Luisa past. Then Rezek stopped, and the girl heard Zdenko's voice: "So that's the famous Hunger Tower. The knight Dalibor learned how to play the violin in there, out of sheer yearning. That was here, wasn't it?"

"Yes," Rezek replied, "but I always think he must have known how to play the violin before. Yearning rarely sings."

And there they stood at the heavy-studded door of the grey tower. Luisa looked up and saw that the thick walls were only partly covered by a newly-built roof. On the open edge of the battlements a slender acacia sapling rose next to a ruffled carline thistle, lifting its pale clusters of leaves into the bright sky with frail grace. That was the last image of the day. It grew damper and darker, and the musty air hung like a veil before the girl's eyes. "Is she still following us?" she heard the student ask. He held his hand out to her. His voice came rough and strange from the indistinct depths of the vault, and Luisa was unable to reply. She groped along the icy walls, holding her breath and thrilling slightly, unable to orient herself until she was met by a reddish light which came, almost warmingly, from the next hall. There she found the two men and the woman bent over something in the middle of the room, and a smoldering candle swayed on a rope just above their bowed heads. Then, with a screech, the light glided further and further down past the three faces, illuminating them harshly for a moment; it sank to their feet and slowly vanished into a round black opening in the floor, over which a last fading gleam flickered. Then Luisa leaned over too and saw the candle, very small, reach a second grey chamber far below, beneath which a third, black chamber seemed to begin.

"Oh," said Luisa.

Zdenko took her moist, trembling hand: "Careful, Luisa."

And then the old woman recited something in a poor, monotonous voice which fluttered in shy circles close above their heads, seeming to fear the damp walls. "The new ones," she was saying, quietly and secretly, as if it were her own precious memory which she was confiding to someone for the first time, "the new ones who came down here got a piece of bread and a pitcher of water. Yes, and with that bread and the water they had to sustain themselves, and there at that hole they had to sit and watch how the ones who had already sat there a week or two weeks, depending (some people have so much stubborn strength), slowly starved to death. Well, and then when it was over in God's name they were let down..."

"On this rope?" Zdenko teased.

The woman was unperturbed: "They were let down, and first they had to push the dead man, the one they had just seen starve to death, into the hole in the floor over there – look." (All of them leaned over.)

"Sometimes they must have half-eaten their predecessors," Rezek laughed cruelly.

"Could be," grumbled the old woman, and went on with her long-accustomed explanation.

Luisa leaned against her brother. "Is it deep?" she probed.

"Very deep."

"And could no one escape?"

"No," Rezek explained. "The place is like a bottle: narrow at the top and sloping out to the floor. There's no climbing out of that. As a matter of fact, it would be the best treatment for the overfed today too."

Luisa heard him laugh. The caretaker pulled the candle up halfway and then stepped back into the room. The men followed her. Here and there the wary, fleeting light of a match opened up unexpected niches and passageways which seemed to collapse again silently a moment later. A vague stirring began. The light over the crater grew fearful, and the vast darkness all around seemed to wake, stretch, and flood past Luisa in burgeoning forms. With increasing vividness she saw couple after couple. And they fell into a reeling dance, and out of the swaying and swirling the One at last revealed himself to her astonished eyes: Julius Caesar.

He was mute and black. Her heart beat in her throat; frightened, she looked down – down,

down into endless depths. She knew: Thus she had stood at the edge of the tower. She herself was the maiden in blue. Her shivering told her that she was unclothed, completely unclothed. She groped down her body with trembling fingers and felt its naked smoothness. Then she looked up: above was night, starless. And then he stood next to her, almost in front of her, on the brink of the abyss. And she raised her hands involuntarily and thrust them straight out at him – until they pressed against his shoulders – but then, in the moment of the sudden contact, she seized him spasmodically, tore him back toward her, felt him, and she swooned in a new, deep, trembling bliss.

And in the end, it seems, the sullen Rosalka was right to consider Zdenko's endeavors and his mother's ambitious desire vainglorious and sinful. For it must have been something like vainglory that moved the young man to change his abode three times within three weeks, namely: from his little room overlooking the walls of the Church of the Order of Malta to prison, from there to the hospital, and finally to the VII. Cemetery of the Wolschan[39], where his mother bought him a piece of land three yards long and two across. That was all he wanted. And all this went so quickly that the old woman, with her

---

[39] Cemetery of the Wolschan: old form of Olschan Cemeteries (Czech *Olšanské hřbitovy*): Large area of cemeteries on what was once the grounds of a Benedictine monastery. The New Jewish Cemetery, where Franz Kafka is buried, is one of the Wolschan's ten cemeteries.

aging mind, could not reconcile herself to this sudden, unexpected elevation in rank; all she could do was shake her head and keep returning to the strange little estate as if incapable of grasping that its new owner liked it out there. Forgetting to work and eat, she went back to the hospital doctor every three days until he finally wearied of explaining the sad case of fatal pneumonia over and over again to the distraught mother and adding that it was no wonder in this foul autumn weather. Every time Mrs. Wanka stepped back out into the dull pearl-grey, dripping day, all but pushed out the door by the impatient doctor and the waiting patients, she always meant to take a good look at the weather in the hopes of understanding the "sad case". But outside she hastened timidly past the buildings and the people and came breathless into the apartment, where she found Luisa, always in the same place, with hot dry eyes and feverish hands. They would sit face to face then without lighting the lamp, without exchanging a word, very far apart, until it was so dark that they forgot about each other. From time to time one of the women would rise and go on tip-toe, as if the other was not supposed to notice, into Zdenko's long-abandoned, dusty little room. She would enter cautiously. And when she found the empty desk and the neglected, shrouded bed, only then would the crazed smile of a wild, ever-credulous hope die on her twitching lips. But the one left behind would listen then: She heard the door open. And then a weeping, frightened and hopeless, began in the abandoned room. Until one Saturday Rosalka washed out the little room in the back and took the key into her keeping. But the weeping did not cease: in the daytime it filled the two rooms, and every night it seemed to go searching all through the house and would not let the children sleep. And the adults let their lights burn on into the morning; for everyone in the old house wanted to see into the corners of their rooms, secretly glad when the next grey rainy day beat at the panes. When people complained the maidservant Rosalka swore by her soul and her honesty that there was nothing one could do but set out holy water and say the Lord's Prayer; for so it was when someone died with many worldly desires in his heart and without the proper composure and humility. And they prayed while peeling turnips and while washing the dishes, the neighbors prayed, and the peddler woman under the stone arcade prayed as well. And holy water was sprinkled after the two women when they came down the vestibule and the corridors with the slow rhythmic steps they had learned behind the hearse. Mrs. Wanka would often go out and hurry down a few alleys only to return home again without purpose. But Luisa did not stir from her place. She had no fantasies anymore, and in her dreams all the colors had grown as pale as the days outside. Sometimes she counted the drops on the window and listened: something rushed past her like a great river in which broken, unintelligible words drifted, more and more of them, and she thought: as if there had been a flood. Then she started as if someone had called her name, and – began to count all the trickling drops again.

All Soul's Day came. Even the broad streets of the New Town look meditative then. Exquisite, showy wreaths are laid out in the elegant flower shops, and their exotic blossoms cannot smile. The entertainment notices on the advertising pillars are papered over, only the *Landestheater* announces a production of the old graveyard comedy *The Miller and His Child*, and in the art dealers' windows three, four, five dark photographs have been slid in front of the colorful English prints, illustrations for Hermann von Gilm's quiet song of melancholy: "Set down on the table the fragrant mignonette..." The lanterns are lit early along the damply-gleaming "Graben", and fiacres and droshkies still drive past with great palm wreaths on the roof and coach-box, and on some of the streetcars the rear lamp is adorned with a fir garland or even a metal wreath which has ridden out this trip on the Day of the Dead many times before. Over cheerless Zizkov[40] the unbelievably long-necked arc lamps[41] have gone up like many sad

[40] Zizkov (Czech *Žižkov*): Traditional working class neighborhood in Prague whose name is derived from the legendary Hussite general Jan Žižka of Trocnov.

[41] Arc lamps: The electrification of Prague seems to have made a dramatic impression on contemporaries. The city was first lit by electricity in 1894; the power was supplied by a small municipal continuous current generator. The arc lamps referred to here are also mentioned by Franz Kafka, among others: "... When the electrical arc lamps were installed below and when this room was furnished, no housewifely allowances were made for how my room would look at this hour from the sofa with the lights out."

moons, and below, at the gates of the ever-growing park of the dead, is an unfestive crowd of people, of weepy people who press toward their goal in dark longing, of angry people who do not understand the haste of pain, of indifferent, celebrating, laughing and watching people and many others. The paths are hemmed in by the lurking impertinent merchant stalls, and the children in the long procession cling like barbs to the lamps and gingerbread and toys on display, creating constant obstructions. But with the crowd and over it this heavy dense effluvium of sad, tired-smelling flowers, withered leaves, rain-soaked soil and damp clothing, seeming to hold the words in suspension, surges on toward the vast shining park. There the masses disperse among the different avenues, but few really have any intention of quickly reaching the grave they have come to bestow their presents upon. First they want to see the other dear departed in their festive raiment, finding it amusing to stroll past the stone crypts of the eminent, reading the strange long names and delighting in the flowers which blanket the precious marble. Then to peek into the murky burial chapels with the bright, glittering altars before which a moldering little old lady is endeavoring for the second day to convey surviving family members' well-paid Lord's Prayers and Hail Marys to the departed ones who are complete strangers to her. And from this gazing on light and splendor an unconscious, lively gladness steals into the faces of the crowd, standing out strangely against the few wounded dark people who steal shy and black to the edge of the path. Now and then they push aside an onlooker in blind impatience, and he thinks in their wake: Birds of death, what are they doing here?

The VII. Cemetery is somewhat more open and secluded. There is more space here, for only part of the fenced-in land is filled with graves and crypts; the rest is unsuspecting, healthy, well-watered ground whose earlier harvests still show, and which with its idling power has helplessly brought forth a lush, wild, senseless garden. That was a good neighborhood for poor Zdenko Wanka, who was still last in the line of graves along the left-hand wall, as if no one since had dared to die in the vast, abysmally crowded city. The two lonely women were keeping him company now for the second day in a row, and old Rosalka came now and then and reported the beauty and splendor of other graves to their deaf pain. If Zdenko's mound refused to look truly festive, despite all the gilly-flowers, asters and forget-me-nots, it was because the new damp earth, in which the grass seeds had not had time to sprout, always came through the adornments somewhere. The fresh grave seemed to withdraw timidly – like a newcomer to a gathering of people whose manners and ways he does not yet know. Neither could the two guests quite find the language of discourse with the deceased, and so dead Zdenko's first holiday must have been rather on the gloomy side. Mrs. Josephine wept no longer. She sat on one of the little wooden benches which stand at the foot of the graves, seemingly forgetting the damp, alien autumn evening which sank closer and closer about her. The daughter, who looked even smaller and paler than usual in her black cashmere dress, watched, without knowing it, the scene unfolding at a grave across the way. A gaunt, careworn man had just set a little blue lantern and a bouquet of lilies-of-the-valley on the grave, and there was a timid, moving tenderness in his gesture, something of the awkward grace of a young person in love. He straightened up and hugged his weeping three-year-old child to his black, badly-cut Sunday coat, but this gesture broke off harshly, and a trembling, hopeless yearning began to bow him. He struggled with it and kept seeking the child's eyes, perhaps to see what the mother's eyes were like, or to draw a little light and hope from them. But the child wept...

Then a group of black-dressed young men in the national costume, the Tschamara, crowded between Luisa and the two motherless ones. They were mostly students, Wanka's friends and comrades who visited the graves of their comrades and leaders today with political eulogies and songs to raise them above the law of equality which held sway inside these quiet walls. Due to the yearly-renewed resistance with which the vigilant authorities met their undertaking, these demonstrations assumed a loud boastful character which went beyond all heartfelt sympathy; youthful vehemence was not content to quietly lay down its blossoming love. So the rows formed to sing one of the bellicose battle songs at Wanka's grave too, recalling the day of the storm to the one who was now reconciled with everything. For surely the loyal comrade – and Wanka had died in loyalty – would welcome tidings of his brothers' perseverance, he would enter their midst again for a moment when his own words and desires woke above the mound. Yet even as the sign was about to be given, the young men fell out of formation with a hollow murmur. They were suddenly ashamed to shout out their rough fighting song into the deep, sacred pain of these women in black, and the best among them glimpsed eternity. They laid down the big wreath, whose evergreen held cards with their names, at the very end of the grave, as if they sensed that the man who had wandered hand in hand with them this far no longer belonged to them, at least not in his deepest yearnings.

And alone among them Rezek remained behind. He stood there tall and solemn, his arms crossed, only inclining his pale hard face as if in thought. He was perhaps the only one to think that Zdenko had died of ravaged joy, even if he was least able to understand it. He was a severe Savonarola[42] by nature, lighting pyres here and there throughout the country, and dedicated young people came to lay all their riches in the flames: joy and laughter and

[42] Savonarola: The Dominican Girolamo Savonarola (1452-1498) was an uncompromising zealot and moralizer from Ferrara who ruthlessly attacked the moral decadence at the court of Pope Alexander VI.

104

longing. For the fanatic wanted an impoverished, self-abnegating army behind him; he
knew that there is no wilder weapon than des-
peration. And his law found followers even in
this soft Slavic people, which, if it denies the
treasures of its heart, loses itself as well.

Luisa too had timidly laid before him all that
she owned from her dream-dark childhood; he
had not noticed it, for she had not seemed
worth winning over as a comrade-in-arms. And
then Luisa had laid down something else,
something unclear and achingly blissful whose
name she did not know: Rezek had not recognized it, for it was her first, tremulous love. –
As he approached the girl now, he felt perhaps
for the first time that it was not a child he bent
down to, and his eyes instinctively greeted the
woman. But Luisa did not understand him;
like everything else, he was far away from her
and long ago. And so at the same time his eyes
took leave of her, and he made one deep bow,
which Luisa had never seen him do before, and
went. It was almost night by now, and with her
sore eyes Luisa could follow him only to the
next crosses.

In the night of this All Soul's Day there was
no weeping in the house across from the
Church of the Order of Malta. Even before it
was fully light, Mrs. Josephine got up, dressed
more painstakingly than usual, and told her
daughter that she was going to the Obersts
today, since she had missed so many Mondays.
Luisa looked up in weak surprise. Her mother's voice seemed utterly strange to her as she

added that she had no intention of losing this good and prominent house. And she would like Luisa to pick her up, to keep the Meerings in mind of her. Then Mrs. Wanka went. And the whole house gazed like one single stone astonishment after her receding steps, which displayed almost the same energetic nimbleness they had before the tragedy. Indeed this swift, unceremonious recovery after weeks of the most absolute sacrifice had something startling and uncanny. In the two days at her son's grave Mrs. Josephine must have discovered some store of inner strength and energy whose existence she had forgotten all these years. Clearly she put it to use, otherwise Frau von Meering could not have described the mother's pain as insufficiently deep and heart-felt. She had expected to see a broken woman and found her almost stiffly upright, she dearly wanted to be moved and emotional in the face of the eloquent pain and now saw something which at best could be called silent sorrow, confronted with which she felt distinctly and uncomfortably at a loss. On top of that there was the desire to learn from this most reliable source how much of "what was said" was true. The Oberst had brought home some very odd rumors from the "Pike", where the regulars liked to talk politics, stories which involved all the latest political catchwords, and in such a way that it suddenly struck Herr von Meering and his wife as a dubious proposition to harbor members of such a disreputable Czech family under their roof. A solemn family council was held;

pro and con, weighed in all fairness, led to no real decision. The death of the youth led astray inclined the old military man toward lenience, and in the end the matter was decided by the astute observation that only the mother, widow of a princely forester and herself quite respectable, had admittance to the house of Meering von Meerhelm, and that the aforementioned capable widow came into close contact only with the fine linens, which for their part were protected from Czechification by the fact that they came from Rumburg and from democratic influences by the five-pointed noble crown of von Meerhelm (since ten year's time). Thus Mrs. Josephine was received quite warmly, and it was taken for granted that the old washing routine was to be kept up as before. Frau von Meering did not relinquish the silent hope that she would learn more at some future time; she took offense at the fact that this had not transpired at their first meeting, and could not restrain herself from assuring the widow in the most innocent tones of her deep condolences for the tragedy, "whose particular circumstances make it all the more painful." This interjection, which made her seem knowing and initiate, impressed her deeply, and she considered it a fine volley against "these people's selfish lack of forthcomingness".

But Mrs. Wanka had noticed nothing at all, neither the disappointment of the Oberstin nor the dig with which she avenged herself; these days she had so much to turn over in her mind, and the results of her musings now took form in quick succession. First of all a small advertisement appeared in a Bohemian and a German newspaper, offering a respectable young man a quiet, well-furnished room in a peaceful neighborhood. Tracking down this promise, one would have found oneself unexpectedly in the Lesser Quarter – would have asked the peddler woman under the stone arcade for "number 87 new[43]" and received the broad, exhaustive answer that that was the Wankas, up three flights of stairs, and that they were hoping to let to gentlemen now, probably because of the unbelievable misfortune they had suffered. Depending on whether the respectable young man was more young or more respectable, he would hear more or less of the fate of the forester's family in the secluded, chatty darkness of the stone arcade. It is unclear how much Ernst Land knew that November day when he twice risked breaking his neck on the familiar spiral staircase of "87 new" and, after various doors had closed indignantly in his face at his German question, he stood at last in front of old Rosalka, who regarded him with great suspicion. She didn't like him, that she knew immediately. He was "too German" for her. She felt that now and then about a person, without knowing what created this impression, whether it was an excess or a lack. She stared

---

[43] Number 87 new: In Prague the houses were originally numbered within each district in the order in which they were built. As the city grew, the modern method of street numbering was adopted, and today the two forms of house numbers exist side by side.

into the glasses of his fogged pince-nez, unable to find the eyes behind them, and had him repeat the German question twice even though she had already understood it. She was reconciled somewhat when the young man brought out the tale of a room to be let somewhere, in very peculiar Bohemian and with great effort. For five days Land had been repeating this assertion at all kinds of doors, and he was fed to the teeth with all the cooking smells and curses he had gotten for his trouble. As Mrs. Wanka, with whom he could speak German, made no unreasonable demands, and the back room seemed tolerable and quiet, he decided to stay. "I don't make any noise," he said in his rather anxious voice at the end of their talk, "and I won't disturb you. During the day I'm in the shop mostly, and in the evening – my God, then you read a bit and..." "Please, please," said Mrs. Wanka, somewhat embarrassed herself. And in the doorway she turned back slightly. "Pardon me, sir, but might I ask what you are?" A pause. – "A pharmacist," said the young man sadly, gazing into the walls of the Church of the Order of Malta. –

Indeed they did not disturb one another, the Wankas and the young dispenser. They barely saw one another. Luisa avoided him; it pained her too deeply to see a stranger enter Zdenko's room, and she could not understand how her mother could have brought herself to do it. She did not understand her mother at all anymore since the long speech she had given her one evening, much concerning her eternal idleness, still more duty and work. And when Luisa timidly expressed her willingness to go to households or work in a shop, something quite startling happened. "You must aim higher, that's nothing for you," was the gist of the widow's rejoinder. "I should have thought of that in the first place. Why did you take piano lessons in Krummau, then; you came quite far with them. And French. If you hadn't neglected it after we moved to Prague, you could be giving lessons today."

Luisa could hardly believe her ears: "Giving lessons?"

"Indeed. Just recently the Frau Oberstin told me she'd know of a nice situation for you if only you were good with children and had some rudimentary French..." Luisa did not even hear the rest; it was too new and strange, what her mother told her. But often in the evening, when her mother and Rosalka did the accounts in the kitchen and Luisa, already half-undressed, sat on the edge of the bed feeling so small and tired, she would fold her hands and say her first childhood prayer and believe its dear, faded words, that she really was a child still, a little blonde child, and she longed for something like a fond fast shelter over her, and dreamed afterwards of angels with long golden wings.

But for all that her mother really did get her way. Luisa took music and French lessons several hours a day, and her teachers affirmed that she was making good progress. She herself was unaware of it. Slowly she realized that she had once possessed other splendid and magical things – long ago – and the substitute she was now given was poor and cold and bare of all beauty. And she spent one winter in dull, willing submission, with no change but that she grew paler, smaller and quieter. Her steps were barely to be heard now, and how often she frightened the neighbor children by appearing in the middle of the corridor without a creak of the stairs; they usually ran away screaming when the girl stretched her pale hands toward it in timid tenderness. – Thus on the surface it seemed a peaceful time, in which each performed her duty calm and unperturbed. Yet a quiet and implacable struggle went on between the active, capable widow who grew sprier by the day and the resigned girl who was still too astonished to realize what was happening to her and found no other weapon against her mother's ruthless resolve than this unnoticeable, mute wilting which lent her little face such a touching, wistful beauty.

Perhaps Ernst Land saw this beauty, but he did not recognize it. He was afraid of the women, and yet he thought of them many an evening, of some vague image of grace and goodness which now held its sheltering hands over him, now lived timidly and fearfully from his protection and his aid. He had grown up in straitened circumstances in the midst of the city, without siblings, without friends, virtually hounded to adulthood by his old, embittered father who could hardly wait until his son began to earn money. At last he tore the boy out of his studies just as he had begun to enjoy science, and as soon as Ernst was established in a pharmacy and provided for, he felt he had done his duty. "Now you have the whole world before you," old Land would declare with the last pathos he could muster. But the young man seemed to have no desire for this "world before him". His thoughts did not venture out into the new and unknown; when he took his eye off them they returned on a thousand secret paths to the unique extinct beauty of his childhood and knelt down before a small, sad woman. All he knew of her was that she sang soft, Slavic songs and that, around the time he started going to school, she lay in bed in the back room and quite slowly and silently, for perhaps a year, without telling anyone, died. At the time he was almost afraid of her, but when she went away so soon he missed her everywhere, and came to attribute all the good that befell him to her tender love, which he believed watched over his days. That is the fate of children orphaned young: They turn down all the joys which their playmates share care-free and blissful and wind them in silent mourning around and around the one dark image of their longing, which slowly seems to grow clearer, happier, more sympathetic in this frame of touching sacrifices... And because they remain poor, they remain lonely, and because they do not betray their joys, they find no comrades for them. Indeed: those whom no mother has shown the way into the world will search and search and never find the door.

Now that he lived with the Wankas the dispenser sometimes felt, for the first time, that he was home. He liked being in his little room, and he spent his free Sundays at the big desk, lost in heavy clouds of pipe-smoke, reading old books whose yellowed pages made him forget today and tomorrow. No wonder he overheard the soft knock at his door and rose with a start when Luisa came in and stopped timid and irresolute behind the dense tobacco fumes. She was like a dream in her faded, unadorned blue dress, with her big reticent eyes, and because she held flowers in her hand, three little white roses which seemed to nestle against her shyly.

"Oh please, excuse me," she said now in German with a slight Slavic intonation, "I thought you had already gone to eat... I only want..." and now she went past him and slipped the three white roses behind a little half-length portrait of Zdenko which hung on the wall next to the window. Land had often looked at it. Now he saw her hands tremble in painful tenderness, and, all taken up by this looking, he was unable to say or do or think anything. He heard the girl: "His first birthday since he left us," – and then all was as it had been, he stood by himself in the Sunday-still room, and now he could have gone on reading. But he could not. He had to keep looking over at the door as if he were expecting someone, and finally the smoke began to irritate him, and he opened the window to let the air of the clear February day flood in fresh and light. For a moment he felt celebratory, and thought: "I have received highborn guests today: three white roses," and smiled as if in a dream.

In September many return to the city from the forest summers and from the lake. They are no longer used to walking on streets, and suddenly, before they can help themselves, they take their hat in their hand as if in the forest, or they sing to themselves loudly. For: the memories are not asleep in them yet. And when they meet one another they are talkative and expansive. They feel something rise from their telling like the splendor of the last secluded days and spread consolingly over the sultry streets and squares. And the two may say in parting: "You look excellent" – and "How you have changed." And for a moment they smile at each other abashed and grateful.

Luisa had returned as well. Since early spring she had been away: There lies a hot secret land. Glowing flowers regard themselves in black tarns and birds and clouds rush past above. White paths wind their way through the trunks of tall black trees, finding a silent, undulating life in these forests. Figures approach in inscrutable guise, and they can be people with sad faces or with cool, laughing lips. First you think you have heard tell of them and you must remember when and what. But they kiss you, and you recognize them as friends you have loved and forgotten. And in remorse you want to kiss them again. But at your greeting their features grow strange, and they retreat into the vast, tossing forest, or they attack you with cruel, bloody words and ask your heart in return. And it is a land of youth: Children and youths, maidens and young mothers with their aching happiness dance and feel their way along the radiant grounds, and their cheeks are hot with an alien joy. But they do not see each other: for in their eyes there is room for nothing but wonder. When they hear the laments or laughter of the other pilgrims they listen and believe it is the birds or the treetops or the winds. They all have one goal: the mountain of flame at the center of the land. And from there many fail to find the way home.

But Luisa returned slowly, smiling from the land called fever through the gardens of recovery. With hesitation she recognized herself and her mother, who kissed her hands, weeping, and the room, which seemed festooned with the golden, full September light. It was a festive homecoming.

And what days those were since she first went outside. This ongoing reunion and exchange of greetings with all things and all people. And the people smiled, and the things shone so. She went as if past shimmering mirrors which wanted to show her how sturdy and tall she had become. And she knew it. She felt strong and rested. Without speaking of it she began to attend her lessons. She had forgotten nothing, and before Christmas she was able to give a little girl piano lessons herself. The child had a great respect for her teacher, and yet in reality their roles were reversed. Every day the love and devotion of this little creature made a multitude of new joyful sensations stir in Luisa, and to her inward listening the child's questions sounded like wonderful, benedictory answers. And all at once so many things happened to her in these tranquil and uneventful days that she did not find the time to look past yesterday; what lay behind seemed to be one great past and reconciliation from which not a shadow reached into this new rich life.

On Christmas Day Luisa went in to the dispenser.

"I only wanted to ask you, Herr Land, please join us this evening, if you have no other plans."

Ernst Land smiled gratefully. Then he followed the girl's gaze and was overcome with embarrassment. Above Zdenko's portrait were three fresh, white roses.

Luisa reached out her hands to him: "You did that?"

"Always..." and Land, vexed at his own blush, quickly promised to come.

This girl paused again at the door. "You're always so sad, Herr Land."

Land was silent.

"What are you thinking about?" and the look as she asked him that moved him so that he admitted with a weeping in his voice:

"About my mother."

On Christmas Eve a strangely festive mood came over these people. And even afterwards it refused to leave their rooms. Like the faint scent of pine, it clung to all things even as Mrs. Josephine, overcome by sudden weakness, spent the long days in bed. Quietly Luisa took all the little household toils out of her hands, one after the other, so that at last she knew nothing but this silent, twilit holiday behind half-drawn curtains with the singing of the stove and the silvery chiming of the clock. And in the evenings there were soft, reticent exchanges between the two women, and no yesterday was ever mentioned in them; it only trembled still in the sound of the voices: in the mother's voice as a soft, timid plea and in the girl's words as a bright, consoling forgiveness. And this lived on in the deep sobs with which Luisa bent one morning over the mother who had passed from her in peaceful reconciliation, without pain and struggle.

Only a week later Luisa took up her lessons again. All her days were brim-full with the multitude of joyful duties, and even when the nights came over her empty and fearful, she felt that no more malicious perils awaited her even in the darkness of suffering. In the stillness of her recovery she had discovered herself for the first time, and had found herself to be so rich and vast that her most sacred possession was not made more lonely by this loss. Grief only lay like a fine boundary about her smile and her movements and could no longer hinder the waking of her being.

There was much winter left in the February of this year; but in March there was a holiday – the Feast of St. Joseph[44] – which made the

---

[44] The Feast of St. Joseph: This holiday is celebrated on March 19.

whole world go mad. Not only did the snow lie forgotten and despised here and there on hills and railway embankments – a greenness had come over the liberated meadows, and overnight yellow catkins bobbed on long bare rods in the wild, light-chasing wind.

Luisa went out to pray at the noon High Mass in the Church of Loreto[45]. But then, hardly able to say how, she wandered past the enticing carillon of the Capuchins and did not look up until she stood on one of the wide lonely paths past the Orchard and spread out her arms. She felt how much she loved everything around her, how much it all belonged to her, and that this quiet, joyful burgeoning with its secret happiness and its sweet yearning was her fate, not what people desired and stumbled toward in dark yearning.

On her way home the bright flocks of merry people came toward her, and she stopped, smiling, and gazed across the bright, living landscape: It was impossible to believe that all these

[45] Church of Loreto: According to legend, in 1291 the house in Nazareth in which the Archangel Gabriel visited the Virgin Mary to announce the birth of the Savior was carried by angels to the Italian town of Loreto near Ancona. This religious motif was especially popular during the Baroque period, prompting the establishment of places of pilgrimage to promote re-Catholicization after of the Battle of the White Mountain. Contemporaries ascribed the victory to the intervention of the Virgin Mary. Many of these Loreto foundations were financed from the confiscated estates of Protestant nobles. The most famous of the Loreto shrines, the Prague Loreto, was founded in 1626 by the wealthy Countess Bengina Katharina von Lobkowitz. True to the custom of the time, the Italian architect Giovanni Orsi was commissioned to build of the chapel, and Italian artists were entrusted with the stucco work and the sculptures.

laughing crowds would ever find room again in the cramped houses over there. For: each of them has outgrown himself into the shimmering day whose weight he barely feels on his shoulders. And the bright sky casts its golden radiance in such swift abundance over all people and things that they forget to have their everyday shadows, and are themselves light in the glimmering land. –

At this image Luisa thought of Zdenko, without knowing why, and wondered whether in his dark life people had ever come toward him like this, bright and happy.

Then she turned homeward. The people's shadows lay piled grey in the cold, abandoned streets like forgotten workday clothing, seeming to give off a musty smell of winter. Luisa shivered, and at the steep sidewalk's very first mischievous suggestion to run, she obliged happily, and trotted childishly downhill past the ancient palaces whose sullen portal-giants glared down at her. But she was not afraid of them anymore.

Rosalka stood in the door, gesticulating as she told an important piece of news to the neighbor women who clustered around her, taking it in with eager nods. One of them glimpsed Luisa, and they all began to wave and call with impatient vehemence. Several children screamed along with them, and all Luisa finally understood was the word: visitor. That was enough to cause her the greatest astonishment. She dashed up the dark stairs with nothing in her mind but one enormous "Who?" With this curiosity in her eyes she burst into the room where Frau von Meering waited on the sofa stiff and straight in undisguised umbrage. But the greatest astonishment was on the part of the Oberstin, who had brought along her condolences for the latest tragedy and was unable to show this radiant, breathless child a single one of her fine, gracious words of sorrow. She felt a powerful, righteous indignation at this laughing good health and felt just as superfluous as she had the last time. "These people," she thought. "It must run in the family."

By now Luisa had managed to make a few apologies, and courteously asked the lady the reason for her visit. Frau von Meering hastily pressed her handkerchief to her face and sobbed from one of its folds: "Your poor, poor mother."

Hearing no response to this moving statement, the Oberstin looked up and emphasized with stern eyes: "She was a very worthy, upright woman."

Luisa sat there with lowered eyes, seeming to regard the tip of her slender foot. The lady waited a little while longer, and as Luisa still had not begun to weep, she saw that all leniency and sympathy would be lost on this obstinate girl. And, her face expressing that she had already begun to rise, as it were, she added in a bitter voice:

"There is only one thing I wanted to say to you, my child. Surely you have already considered the changes necessitated by your worthy mother's death?"

"I don't know" – Luisa hesitated, perplexed.

"Why, it goes without saying that you must give this young man his notice immediately; I am astonished to find him still living with you."

"But –" went Luisa with big startled eyes. Then an almost mischievous smile flickered across her face.

Frau von Meering was already at the door.

"I considered it my duty to bring it to your attention. Of course you may do as you please."

"Yes, my lady," replied Luisa in a sudden access of high spirits, standing on her toes to match the Oberstin, who seemed to grow taller and taller. Then she asked with a smile: "Won't you take a moment's rest, my lady?"

But the lady fled from this ghastly house. She was already in the kitchen, where the old maidservant Rosalka flung herself at her impetuously, then very carefully kissed the sleeve of her silk mantilla near the elbow. The insulted one tore herself from the slavish obeisance with a curt "Adieu", finding only small recompense for the "abuse she had suffered" in the gapes and whispered admiration of the neighbors on the stairs and in the corridors.

Luisa stood for a while lost in thought. Rosalka went to the front window to catch one last glimpse of the aristocratic lady who, as she emphasized, had been "visiting with us".

She returned with very curious eyes.

Luisa did not notice. Pacing up and down, she said: "I believe we'll stay in this apartment. And I completely forgot to discuss that with you, Rosalka. So now you are in my service, under the same conditions. That is, if you wish?"

The old woman swore her mortal and eternal happiness, and in her tears she suddenly said "Madam" to her mistress instead of "Loisinka", as she had called her since childhood.

Then Luisa knocked on Land's door.

He came up to her with a smile. "You mole!" she cried at him jokingly, "always in your room. Today you must go out into the city. Spring! I was outside, far, far," and she made a gesture as if to show him where Spring lies. Her eyes gleamed with such promise. There she went on in an important, business-like tone: "I don't want to disturb you, Herr Land. I only wanted to tell you this. I am going to keep the apartment; so everything will stay as it was, that is, if you are satisfied with your room otherwise?"

He sought her eyes and then looked quickly at the floor: "Oh," he said softly, "I'm very happy here, I think..." He began to rub his palms together...

Luisa kept her hand on the doorknob: "That's good," she assisted him, now somewhat at a loss herself.

He looked as if he had something on his mind.

The two young people were silent.

Then the girl began: "I would so like to learn some better German, maybe you can use some Bohemian in exchange."

"Yes," said Land with a sigh of relief, "I love your language."

"So," Luisa ordered cheerfully, "then come out to the front room for a while when you have time. There are a few books there, German ones too."

And at the door she added: "Come as often as you like," and more quietly: "You must tell me ever so much about your mother."

Afterword

Rainer Maria Rilke completed his *Two Prague Stories* in the years 1897 and 1898 respectively. They were written, incidentally, in two German cities: in Munich, where Rilke spent two semesters studying the humanities, and in Berlin-Schmargendorf, where he moved after his studies in Munich. By that time the German-Bohemian conflict had long since developed into a (not only) verbal battle in which the rare words of reason or moderation were drowned out by the cries of fanatically nationalistic mobs on both sides.

The budding Czech national consciousness at the beginning of the 19th century was still based on the works of Czech scholars who had written in German, such as the linguist and literary scholar Josef Dobrovský, who is considered the creator of modern Czech. Toward the end of the century, when *Two Prague Stories* were written, such "open-mindedness" had become unthinkable. Political liberalism seemed to have had its day: on the Czech side the "Young Czech" party had formed, not hesitating to enter the parliamentary election in spring 1897 with a radical anti-Semite like Václav Březnovský, while the German-speaking citizens increasingly harked to the nationalistic slogans of the German Nationals.

In 1895, Emperor Franz Joseph had commissioned the former Governor of Galicia, Casimir Count Badeni, to form a "government of the strong hand". The reactions to Badeni's language regulations show that any possibility for dialogue between the two peoples occupying the country was a thing of the past. Badeni, who was supposed to push through the tax legislation while carrying out outstanding budget negotiations with Hungary, attempted to keep peace with the Czechs by making various concessions. Barely a month after coming into office he had lifted the state of emergency which had been declared in Prague two years before. With the suffrage reform which he brought through the Imperial Council in June 1896, he hoped to convince the "Young Czechs", who had been represented in the Vienna Parliament since 1891, to abandon their position of stubborn obstructionism and work constructively as members of parliament. Badeni was forced to realize, however, that only concessions to the Czechs' language demands could bring about the desired results. Thus he enacted language regulations for Bohemia on April 5, 1897 (followed three weeks later by analogous regulations for Moravia), provoking violent reactions, indeed a state crisis.

According to Badeni's regulations, which were enacted without consulting the representatives of the Bohemian Germans, Czech and German were to be given equal status in official transactions in the Bohemian crown lands. Thus, a German official in a German-speaking town such as Reichenberg would have had to learn Czech if he hoped to continue his career in the public service. The implications for the German-speaking population in the areas later called Sudeten-German, in which a large percentage of officials were Czech in the first place, can only be appreciated if one takes into consideration these people's sense of identity and their fears. In addition, they had expected Vienna to support them in the nationalist conflict and now felt that they had been sold out.

The protests and mass demonstrations, whose vehemence surpassed all expectations, not only swept the country's large German towns, such as Reichenberg, Karlsbad and Teplitz, but carried away the German population in all of Austria, all the way to distant alpine Graz. In German regions of Bohemia there were riots against Czech minorities. In the Vienna Parliament, where the parliamentary negotiations had developed into a bitter battle, few qualms were shown – when arguments failed, a manfully-swung fist was still a political option.

In the face of these dangerous developments, Emperor Franz Joseph had no other choice but to close down the parliament on November 28, 1897 and dismiss Badeni.

That December the tension exploded in the streets of Prague, resulting in violent anti-German and anti-Semitic riots. The Young Czech politicians – unlike the Social Democrats – stood idly by. Only the imposition of martial law ended this anarchic madness of the streets.

Rilke must have heard these battle cries from across the German border after he left his birth city of Prague in 1896 at the age of 21. In Prague, after his school-leaving examinations, Rilke had made brief attempts to study the humanities (literature, history, philosophy, art) before taking up law in accordance with his parents' wishes. He had already begun working on the two stories "King Bohusch" and "The Siblings" as a way of declaring his sympathies in the struggle between the Czech and the German nationalities. The Prague German Rilke's clear support of the Czechs can only be understood if one grasps the youthful force which the Czech emancipation movements manifested around the turn of the century. Only a few decades before, the rapid demise of the Czech language had been prophesied; at best, it was thought, it would become a dialect spoken only by a few peasants. In Rilke's youth these gloomy prognoses had long since given way to a brilliant renaissance. The remarkable achievements of the Czech culture had begun to ensure it an equal position alongside other European cultures, or at least allowed it to emphatically demand this status.

The young student Rilke sympathized with the group which (at first) seemed weaker, though he overlooked the fact that this party, the Czechs, had long since ceased to be a powerless, prostrate people. Old newspapers testify to the quite inflammatory resolutions of the Prague City Council, where the Czechs were already in the majority, for example with regard to the use of the German language; it is difficult to deny that the victim role insisted on to this day is somewhat far-fetched. The German population of Prague was in the retreat; the fears of the Germans (many of whom, incidentally, were Jewish) that they might be "driven" from the city even with the Viennese Imperial House behind them are understandable in the context of the demographic development and the constant attempts to take politics onto the streets.

But other factors as well suggest that Rilke's position in this conflict was determined by his age.

A hypothesis which sheds more light on his position is that the young Rilke, barely out of puberty, was attempting to reject the world of his – German – parents by taking the side of the Czechs. Rilke's biographers have reported noteworthy things about his family; in particular he seems to have had a difficult relationship with his affected mother Phia Rilke. She (like her son, incidentally) was plagued by an obsession with the aristocracy and initially raised her "little lad" René Karl Wilhelm Johann Josef Maria as a girl.

In the issue of nationalities Rilke could rebel against his fanatically German mother, whose snobbery prevented her from understanding her son's position; she could not even reconcile herself to the fact that René learned "Bohemian" in school. In "The Siblings" Rilke lent the aristocratic wife of the Oberst a. D. Meering von Meerhelm (noble "since ten years time") unmistakable traits of his mother.

Rilke's German compatriots were equally disgruntled at the "betrayal" of the young man, who after all continued to move in the circles of the German "Concordia" (Association of German Writers and Artists in Bohemia) and the Association of German Fine Artists. The Trautenau literary historian Josef Mühlberger reports the "national indignation toward the cultural sin committed with the language of our archenemy by a writer who calls himself a German." However, it is impossible to exaggerate the credit due to a German (or, if you will, though it is not in Rilke's spirit, Austrian) writer who addressed himself to the concerns of the Czechs in these turbulent years. In this context the literary shortcomings of the two stories, in particular "The Siblings", which bristles with dialectics, pale before the value of the whole. And it continues to be of value for all readers interested in more than a superficial black-and-white sketch of the complex German-Czech conflict in Prague.

Harald Salfellner

Contents

Foreword by Rainer Maria Rilke 3

King Bohush 5

The Siblings 64

Afterword 124